Amber

Annabelle Starr

Illustrated by Helen Turner

EGMONT

Special thanks to:

Rachel Rimmer, St John's Walworth Church of England
School and Belmont Primary School

EGMONT

We bring stories to life

Amber first published in Great Britain 2008
by Egmont UK Limited
239 Kensington High Street, London W8 6SA

Text & illustration © 2008 Egmont UK Ltd
Text by Rachel Rimmer
Illustrations by Helen Turner

ISBN 978 1 4052 3932 5

1 3 5 7 9 10 8 6 4 2

A CIP catalogue record for this title is available
from the British Library

Typeset by Avon DataSet Ltd, Bidford on Avon, Warwickshire
Printed and bound in Great Britain by the CPI Group

Meet the
Megastar Mysteries Team!

Hi, I'm **Rosie Parker**, mystery-solving aide to the stars and these are my partners against crime . . .

. . . **Soph** (Sophie) **McCoy** – this girl's so fashion-forward she's in the next century – and . . .

. . . **Abs** (Abigail) **Flynn** – homework buff and mastermind extraordinaire!

If Soph's fashion-forward, my mum, **Liz Parker**, is fashion-backward; her outfits are stuck in the 1980s along with her music taste. She's cringey, she's sooo not cool, but I do love her . . .

. . . and last but by no means least, meet my nan, **Pam Parker**. I have to admit, her obsession with murder-mystery shows does come in handy from time to time (although the garibaldis I can do without . . .)

Consider yourself introduced!

ROSIE'S MINI MEGASTAR PHRASEBOOK

Want to speak our lingo, but don't know your soeurs from your signorinas? No problemo! Just use my comprehensive guide . . .

-a-rama	add this ending to a word to indicate a large quantity: e.g. 'The after-show party was celeb-a-rama'
amigo	Spanish for 'friend'
au contraire, mon frère	French for 'on the contrary, my brother'
au revoir	French for 'goodbye'
barf/barfy/barfissimo	sick/sick-making/very sick-making indeed
bien sûr, ma soeur	French for 'of course, my sister'
bon	French for 'good'
bonjour	French for 'hello'
celeb	short for 'celebrity'
convo	short for 'conversation'
cringe-fest	a highly embarrassing situation
Cringeville	a place we all visit from time to time when something truly embarrassing happens to us
cringeworthy	an embarrassing person, place or thing might be described as this
daggy	Australian for 'unfashionable' or 'unstylish'
doco	short for 'documentary'
exactamundo	not a real foreign word, but a great way to express your agreement with someone
exactement	French for 'exactly'

excusez moi	French for 'excuse me'
fashionista	'a keen follower of fashion' – can be teamed with 'sista' for added rhyming fun
glam	short for 'glamorous'
gorge/gorgey	short for 'gorgeous': e.g. 'the lead singer of that band is gorge/gorgey'
hilarioso	not a foreign word at all, just a great way to liven up 'hilarious'
hola, señora	Spanish for 'hello, missus'
hottie	no, this is *not* short for hot water bottle – it's how you might describe an attractive-looking boy to your friends
-issimo	try adding this ending to English adjectives for extra emphasis: e.g. coolissimo, crazissimo – très funissimo, non?
je ne sais pas	French for 'I don't know'
je voudrais un beau garçon, s'il vous plaît	French for 'I would like an attractive boy, please'
journos	short for 'journalists'
les Français	French for, erm, 'the French'
Loserville	this is where losers live, particularly evil school bully Amanda Hawkins
mais	French for 'but'
marvelloso	not technically a foreign word, just a more exotic version of 'marvellous'
massivo	Italian for 'massive'
mon amie/mes amis	French for 'my friend'/'my friends'
muchos	Spanish for 'many'

non	French for 'no'
nous avons deux garçons ici	French for 'we have two boys here'
no way, José!	'that's never going to happen!'
oui	French for 'yes'
quelle horreur!	French for 'what horror!'
quelle surprise!	French for 'what a surprise!'
sacrebleu	French for 'gosh' or even 'blimey'
stupido	this is the Italian for 'stupid' – stupid!
-tastic	add this ending to any word to indicate a lot of something: e.g. 'Abs is braintastic'
très	French for 'very'
swoonsome	decidedly attractive
si, si, signor/signorina	Italian for 'yes, yes, mister/miss'
terriblement	French for 'terribly'
une grande	French for 'a big' – add the word 'genius' and you have the perfect description of Abs
Vogue	it's only the world's most influential fashion magazine, darling!
voilà	French for 'there it is'
what's the story, Rory?	'what's going on?'
what's the plan, Stan?	'which course of action do you think we should take?'
what the crusty old grandads?	'what on earth?'
zut alors!	French for 'darn it!'

Hi Megastar reader!

My name's Annabelle Starr*. I'm a fashion stylist – just like Soph's Aunt Penny – which means it's my job to help celebrities look their best at all times.

Over the years, I've worked with all sorts of big names, some of whom also have seriously big egos! Take the time I flew all the way to Japan to style a shoot for a girl band. One of the members refused to wear the designer number I'd picked out for her and insisted on sporting a dress her mum had run up from some revolting old curtains instead. The only way I could get her to take it off was to persuade her it didn't match her pet Pekingese's outfit!

Anyway, when I first started out, I never dreamt I'd write a series of books based around my crazy celebrity experiences, but that's just what I've done with Megastar Mysteries. Rosie, Soph and Abs have just the sort of adventures I wish my friends and I could have got up to when we were teenagers!

I really hope you enjoy reading the books as much as I enjoyed writing them!

Love **Annabelle**

* I'll let you in to a little secret: this isn't my real name, but in this business you can never be too careful!

Chapter One

It was a wet Saturday afternoon, I had a massive zit on my nose and huge piles of homework to do. Yet this was possibly one of the most exciting days of my life! No, I wasn't in some kind of parallel universe, like in *Doctor Who*. I was excited because me, Soph and Abs were about to win a radio competition to meet The Gems!

The Gems were this totally hot new band from near Borehurst. The three girls in the band talked Girl Power, but you knew they really meant it; they wouldn't stab each other in the back over a hot boy. These girls were mates, through and through – they had been since the first day of school, kind of like me, Abs and Soph. Maybe that's why we liked them. Anyway, we were totally about to win – live on air!

'Stop hogging the phone,' Abs hissed at me. The three of us were squidged together on my bed, trying to listen to my mobile.

'Owww!' shrieked Soph as her humongous silver clip-on earring got caught in my phone charm.

'Sssh!' I said, untangling her. 'We won't hear when they call us!'

'Let's go to line two, to Rosie, Sophie and Abs!' the DJ said. 'Hello there!'

I gave a mini-scream as Abs and Soph calmly said, 'Hello.'

'So, you want to win a chance to interview The Gems, do ya?' he asked. 'Live on Fleetwich FM – the focal vocals for all funky folks!'

I rolled my eyes. Why do all local radio DJs have to be so cheesy? 'Yes please!' I said politely.

'Right! Well, answer this question: where did The Gems get their name?'

We looked at each other. This was so easy. 'Amber is a type of gem, and she's the lead singer,' Abs said coolly.

There was a pause. 'So, you're saying it's cos the lead singer's name is a kind of gemstone . . .?' the DJ began.

Hel-*lo*? Wasn't that what Abs said? 'Yes!' I said firmly.

'Well,' he said. 'I can tell you that . . .'

We were squeezing each other's hands.

'. . . you're right!!' he finally shouted.

We dropped the phone and leapt up, squealing and laughing. We'd won! We were going to meet The Gems!!

Soph did a mad dance involving lots of kicking legs (not ideal, as both her shoes flew off and hit me and Abs). Abs jumped up and down. I just screamed and screamed.

'Rosie, what is going on?' Mum had appeared at my bedroom door. She stared at Abs and Soph, who were now hugging each other.

'I thought there'd been a murder!' Nan said from behind Mum, panting from rushing upstairs.

I shook my head, too out of breath to explain.

'I guess that means you're happy. Ha ha!' the DJ quacked from my mobile, abandoned on the bed. 'Fleetwich FM aims to please . . .'

We all scrabbled for the phone.

'Hello, hi, sorry about that!' I gabbled, waving madly at Abs and Soph to shut the door and get rid of Mum and Nan.

'Well done!' the DJ cried cheerily. 'Stay on the line and we'll make arrangements. Here's the latest song from The Gems themselves – "Crystal Clear".'

As it started to play, he transferred me to a producer and I gave her my details. By this time, Soph and Abs were back.

'The interview will be next Saturday at eleven a.m.,' the producer said.

'Next Saturday at eleven,' I repeated, looking at Soph and Abs. Abs nodded immediately, but

Soph looked agonised before nodding too. 'Great! See you then. Thanks!'

'What's up, Soph?' I asked, ringing off.

'I'm supposed to be working next Saturday.'

Soph has this weekend job in Dream Beauty, a beauty salon in Borehurst. She's always moaning about it but she needs the money. She is obsessed with clothes. Not your common-or-garden designer gear – her own creations. She gets stuff from charity shops and customizes it in totally bizarre ways that somehow work (on her, anyway). Stuff from charity shops doesn't exactly cost the earth, but let's just say Soph can buy a LOT on a shopping trip. Never underestimate the fashionista-sista side of her.

'Can't you get the day off?' Abs asked.

'I have to, but Mrs Blessing will kill me,' Soph said.

'Well, you work on her, and I'll persuade Mum to drive us,' I said. 'Oh, hi, Mum.'

She'd opened the door again. 'That was pretty loud screaming, girls. How do you fancy being backing singers for the Banana Splits?'

I shuddered. Mum's Bananarama tribute band is cringe-worthy enough without actually performing with them. But if that was what it would take to get her to drive us to Fleetwich FM, I'd leap into some spandex leggings in a heartbeat.

* * *

On Wednesday morning, Soph was beaming. 'I've got the day off on Saturday!'

'How'd you wangle that?' I asked.

'I'm working the next three Fridays after school.'

'Brilliant!' Abs said.

Just then, Amanda Hawkins the class witch sneered into view. 'Are the Tragic Trio having fun?'

'We're just talking about meeting The Gems on Saturday,' Abs said. 'Cos we won that competition. To meet The Gems.'

'Whatever,' Amanda said, storming off. 'Losers.'

'Er, winners, I think you'll find,' I called after her. Somehow, Amanda being hacked off made me even happier.

The Gems were even mentioned in *Star Secrets* that week. They'd been at a party with Poppy Carlton, the winner of *Teen Town*, the teen reality show that was massive last summer. She's always in the goss mags, partying and clubbing, even though she's only sixteen. Soph is sooo jealous of her because she's always got the latest hot bag or shoes. The Gems were hitting the big time!

✳ ✳ ✳

That Saturday, thanks to my marvelloso persuasive powers (and promising to go to the next Banana Splits gig), Mum was driving me, Abs and Soph to Fleetwich FM. Unfortunately, she was also singing along to the radio très loudly.

'You know I want yoooo-ou, you know I need yoooo-ou!'

'Mu-um!'

Abs and Soph winced in sympathy.

'You're the only one! You're no lonely one!'

I tried to turn the radio down.

'Ooh no, I like this one, Rosie. Leave it on. Ah, here we are.'

Sacrebleu.

We turned up a lane that led to a large building. It looked totally ordinary. Who'd have thought some soon-to-be megastars were waiting inside – for us!

'Come on!' Soph was already out of the car.

'Call me when you're done,' Mum said.

Nervously, we walked into the totally featureless reception area.

'Er, we're here to interview The Gems,' I said to the security guard. 'We're the winners. You know, of the competition. On Fleetwich FM. Obviously.'

'Sign there, please,' he said in a bored tone. He told us to take the lift to the fifth floor.

It was a bit livelier up there. Music pumped from speakers and as the lift doors opened, a funky-looking girl in shorts and boots approached us.

'I'm Jenny. Are you the competition-winners?'

'Yup!' Abs said.

'Follow me. You're on in fifteen minutes.'

We followed Jenny down the corridor and into a room filled with comfy sofas.

'Danny Darwin will be ready for you soon,' Jenny said.

We sat down to wait.

'So, have you got your list of questions, Rosie?' Abs asked.

'Bien sûr, ma soeur,' I replied. A good journalist – which is what I'm going to be one day – is always prepared. I opened my notebook.

Question One, it said. And that was all. I remembered now – Nan had called me to sort out the Sky Plus for her and I'd never carried on! Aargh.

Abs and Soph were looking at me expectantly. I could see they'd both written loads.

'Er, yes,' I said. 'Lots of questions here.' Well, a good journalist also knows how to think on her feet.

Just then, there was a knock on the door. The Gems had arrived! Amber, the lead singer, bounded in first. She had long blonde hair and wore jeans and a funky yellow top. Rachel and Carly weren't far behind. They both wore très cool shirtdresses, one white, one green. Rachel had short brown hair and Carly had her black hair scraped back in a ponytail. They all grinned as they shook our hands.

'Nice to meet you,' Amber said.

'It's such a pleasure to meet you,' I gushed.

'I love your hairband,' Amber said to Soph, who beamed. She'd added some sequins to an Alice band and it was her new fave thing to wear.

'It's really cool we're being interviewed by three friends,' Rachel said.

'Yeah,' Carly agreed. 'It's so appropriate!'

'Right, in you come, girls,' Jenny said. 'This way.'

We all followed Jenny to a door marked Studio 1. Behind it was a large room with a massive desk covered in buttons and slidey things and lights.

I seriously wanted to fiddle with them, but realised a serious journalist would not behave like an idiot. Chairs stood around a table with a microphone on it. Danny Darwin, the DJ, took off his headphones to say hello.

Jenny showed us where to sit at the table. Amber smiled at me as I sat next to her. She was so nice!

Danny turned the music down. 'And in two minutes we'll be talking to The Gems, so stay tuned!' Then he flicked a switch and some adverts came on. 'Right, ladies,' he said, turning to us. 'Ready?'

We looked at each other and nodded. My throat had suddenly got very dry.

'So, here we are with The Gems,' Danny said, 'and our competition-winners, Sophie, Abs and Rosie are running the show. Take it away, girls!'

'So,' I said nervously, 'how long have you been in the band?'

'A few years,' Rachel replied. 'Since we left school, we've been playing at youth clubs, shopping centres and school fêtes.'

'And now we've got a deal with this massive record label!' Carly said.

Amber looked at her mates. 'Yup. They say we're going to be huge.' She didn't look happy though.

'Did they hear you play somewhere?' Abs asked.

'Our manager – Amber's dad – had sent them a demo CD. A scout came to watch us at the mall in Borehurst,' Rachel said.

Soph was next. 'If you were an item of clothing, what would you be?'

The Gems looked a little startled. Then they grinned.

'Ballet pumps,' Carly said. 'They're girly and sweet, like me!'

'I'd be a charm bracelet,' Rach said. 'It's dainty and looks good on someone's arm.'

Amber snorted and tried to turn it into a cough.

'Ooh, whose arm would you like to be on?' I asked Rach quickly.

'Well, mine, obviously,' Danny interjected. The girls all laughed.

'How about you, Amber?' Soph asked.

'I'd have to say some vintage boots. Because I'm individual, hard-working and totally rock 'n' roll.'

I couldn't help thinking it was an odd thing for a member of a pop group to say.

Abs chimed in with her next question, but I was distracted. There was definitely something weird about Amber. Why did I feel that The Gems weren't such close friends after all?

Chapter Two

The interview was a success! Afterwards, The Gems all beamed at us, and Danny Darwin shook our hands.

'I'd better watch out for my job!' he joked. 'You girls thought up some great questions.'

Me, Abs and Soph grinned at each other. I had to admit, it did all add up to a pretty cool interview, what with Abs asking The Gems about their musical influences, Soph asking fashion questions and me finding out which celebs they'd met and who were their heroes.

'We work pretty well together, don't we?' I said to the girls as we left the studio.

'You sure do,' Rachel said, overhearing me. 'Like us! It's so cool when you know each other so well, you know what the other girls are thinking.'

Amber stared at her and opened her mouth to say something, then closed it again.

Carly was nodding. 'Yeah. Mates from school are the best!'

'Totally,' said Abs. She turned to me and Soph. 'We'll always be friends, won't we?'

Soph grinned. 'Si, si, signorina,' she said.

'Bien sûr, ma soeur,' I said. 'Although, Soph, if the fashion item *you* would be was anything from the eighties, I'd have to reconsider.'

Soph pretended to punch my arm. The Gems laughed.

We were at the lifts again. Was it time to go already? I hadn't even called Mum to fetch us.

'Well, our manager's waiting for us. We should go. Those hit songs won't write themselves, you know!' Carly said.

Amber fidgeted and looked at her feet.

'They certainly won't,' Rach agreed. 'Great to meet you all. Catch you at a gig some time? We're playing Fleetwich shopping centre next week.'

'Definitely!' me, Abs and Soph all chorused, waving as the lift doors closed behind The Gems.

'Well,' Soph said, 'that was brillissimo!'

'Yeah!' Abs said. 'I'm gutted we have to go now, though. Rosie, have you called your mum? . . . Hello, earth to Rosie?'

'Sorry? Oh, right, yeah. Will do. I was just thinking, did you notice that Amber was looking uncomfortable? Once when Rach mentioned knowing what your friends were thinking, and then when Carly said they wrote hit songs?'

'Nope,' Soph said. 'What are you on about?'

'She looked like you'd look if someone said my mum was more fashion-savvy than you. Totally gutted,' I insisted. 'Didn't you notice? I wonder what's wrong?'

'Will you just stop with your mystery radar?' Abs asked. 'She probably remembered she hadn't fed her goldfish or something. Now please call your mum.'

I got out my phone, sighing. Amber didn't have a goldfish. I'd read enough celebrity gossip to know that much for certain. Something definitely wasn't right with The Gems, despite them saying what good friends they were.

Mum said she'd be ten minutes, so we hung around on the fifth floor, not wanting to wait in the boring reception. Jenny said we could look round the offices, so we wandered through. It was mostly desks with computers on them, and there weren't many people there (duh! – it was Saturday!), but a friendly girl wearing a huge jumper waved at us. We headed straight over to talk to her in case she had some radio goss to share.

'Hey, girls. Loved your interview just now!' she said.

'Thanks,' I said.

'I'm Judy. I do the traffic reports.'

'Right,' said Soph, looking round for someone else to talk to.

'I'm not normally in the office much – I spend a lot of time in the traffic helicopter – so I'm just catching up on stuff today. Glad I did – I got to meet The Gems.'

'Yeah, they're nice, aren't they?' But I was suddenly more excited about Judy's job. 'So you get to go in a helicopter?' How cool was that, even if you did have to talk about traffic. At least you were on the radio, in a helicopter!

Judy laughed. 'It's not as glamorous as it sounds! But it's good fun. You should come along some time. See the world from the sky!'

'Seriously?' asked Abs.

'Yeah, why not? It'd be a tight squeeze, but you might get a chance to join in with the report. It'd be fun.'

I wasn't convinced doing traffic reports was my idea of 'fun'. Still, a ride in a helicopter would be cool!

'We'd love to!' I said quickly, before she could change her mind. 'Thanks!'

'Let me take your details and I'll give you a call

when there's a chance for you to join us. We like to liven things up for our listeners here at Fleetwich FM.'

Cool-a-rama! We were going to fly in a helicopter! What a brilliant day.

* * *

Everyone at school must have got totally sick of us going on about The Gems and the radio station that week. We did mention it quite a bit. Even Mr Lord was pretending he'd heard of them by the end of our drama lesson.

'Make like a Gem and glow, Rosie! I want to see your inner radiance!' he shouted at me. Honestly, how a peasant is supposed to have inner radiance, I don't know. They didn't exactly have moisturiser back in the fourteenth century or whenever, did they?

Anyway, it turns out we gave The Gems some good publicity, cos by Friday, quite a crowd from our year were planning to see them playing in Fleetwich shopping centre the next day. Abs had even heard Amanda Hawkins saying to Lara and Keira, her evil cronies, that she might go along, 'to see what all the fuss is about'. Ha, trust Amanda to have to be in on *everything*. I bet she thought some talent scouts would be there and might spot her. Sadly, her talent is in short supply. Unless you can have a career in evil hair-flicking, I think she'll be disappointed.

Poor old Soph was working, but luckily for her the gig started at half-past six, so she just had time to zoom home, take off her minging salon uniform and transform herself into the fashionable Soph we know and love. I don't know how she did it in just fifteen minutes, but Abs pointed out she'd probably been planning her outfit all week.

Anyway, we got to the gig in plenty of time to get a good position at the front of the crowd. There were loads of people milling about. We saw Frankie and Becky from our year and waved, but they couldn't get past an enormous group of excited ten-year-olds, so they gave up on trying to join us.

The Gems came on stage wearing really cute matching skirts and tops. We all shrieked when we saw them. Carly and Rachel looked totally professional – all poised with their headphone-style microphones by their mouths. I thought Amber looked nervous at first, but once they launched into 'Crystal Clear', I forgot all about her as we jumped about and sang along. They had a dance routine and everything – they were real, live pop stars!

After they'd finished their set and left the stage, me, Abs and Soph hid behind a large plant near the escalators. It was my idea to hang around, hoping we could say hi to them. After all, we did know them – we were practically their *friends*. Everyone else was slowly leaving, being hassled by the security guards, who wanted to close the shopping centre. I watched Amanda Hawkins protesting as one of them took her by the elbow and prepared to shove her out.

'Hey, look!' Abs suddenly hissed, digging me in the ribs.

I turned to see The Gems coming out of a door marked 'Private' and before I knew what I was doing, I leapt out from behind the plant and waved at them. The bloke with them didn't look very amused at this, but the girls all grinned and came straight over to talk to us. They'd changed out of their stage outfits, but were still perfectly co-ordinated in jeans and tops.

'Hi!' Carly said.

'That was fantastic!' Soph said.

'Yeah, you really got everyone dancing!' I said.

Rachel laughed. 'Even though our routine went a bit wrong at one point?'

'I've told you about that,' the bloke said. 'You need to practise more, girls.' He was looking at Amber sternly. She flushed.

'This is our manager, Barry,' Carly said. 'Amber's dad. He got us our record deal. We pretty much owe everything we've achieved so far to him.'

Amber coughed a little and folded her arms, but Barry didn't notice. He was beaming at Carly.

'Pleased to meet you, Barry,' Abs said promptly, sticking her hand out to shake his. That's what I love about Abs – she's so good with parents. She always knows how to butter them up.

Amber's dad shook her hand. 'It's Mr Smith to you girls,' he said rather sternly. Then he smiled a bit. 'So you're the ones who interviewed The Gems last week? Interesting . . . er . . . questions.'

'Well, *we* enjoyed it, didn't we, Carly? Rach?' Amber said quickly.

'Yeah,' they both replied, beaming.

'Right, come on, girls,' Barry said. 'It's early to bed tonight. You've got to be fresh for the photo shoot tomorrow. Dark circles under the eyes are *not* part of your look – at least, that's not what I've told the make-up artist.' He laughed as if he'd said something funny, and put his arms round Amber and Carly, steering them away from us. Rach followed them.

'Bye!' she called, waving.

'Is it me or is their manager a bit weird?' Soph asked as we watched them walk away. 'I mean, whoever heard of someone's dad worrying about make-up?'

'His grip was très firm,' said Abs, rubbing her hand. 'He's clearly someone who means business.'

'Uh-oh,' I said. 'Here comes trouble.'

A cross-looking security guard was marching towards us across the deserted shopping centre. We grinned at him and made a dash for the door.

* * *

After seeing The Gems twice in a week, we didn't see them for months and months. Boring-hurst really lived up to its name. Even seeing Lucy Cameron and Ben Taylor snogging outside Top Choonz didn't make us raise an eyebrow. (And what's so romantic about standing outside Top Choonz anyway? I just don't get it. I mean, if it was someone like Orlando Bloom, I would understand. You'd want to snog him wherever you were. But Ben from maths? Weirdissimo.) Anyway, we did see The Gems quite a lot in a way – in the pages of *Star Secrets* and other celebrity mags. It seemed they were really getting out and about, invited to all the best parties and premières. They were forever in the fashion pages too. Soph pored over their outfits.

'They're always so cool,' she said admiringly.

'They're always wearing the same thing as each other though,' Abs pointed out. 'Isn't that a bit unimaginative?'

Sophie sighed heavily. 'It's called *styling*, Abs. They are a pop group, and they have a certain look. Therefore they have to look similar. Duh.'

About two months after the gig at the shopping centre, I sauntered into the newsagent's to get my copy of the latest *Star Secrets*. I couldn't believe my eyes. Amber from The Gems was over all the front covers of all the goss mags! 'Amber vs Poppy!' one cover said. '"She's a Waste of Space!" claims pop star,' said another. *Star Secrets* had the words 'Gems Spark Row!' splashed over a picture of Amber and Poppy. Zut alors! I grabbed it and flicked to the main story so I could find out what was going on.

As it turned out, The Gems had been at the premiere of the Sweetland twins' latest film. Some journalist had made a comment about the so-called 'stars' that were there, and Amber had agreed.

'Listen to this,' I said to Soph and Abs as soon as I got hold of them at break. '"I don't know why Poppy Carlton's even famous," the blonde member of The Gems said. "She doesn't *do* anything."'

'Oooh, nasty!' Soph said.

'Well, we know she's suddenly speaking her mind,' Abs said. 'Remember her comment about eighties music last week?'

I winced. 'My mum's still going on about that. She's très outraged Amber said all eighties pop music was rubbish. She keeps saying, "She's obviously never heard of Wham! 'Club Tropicana' – now *that* was a great song." Me and Nan are going to strangle her if she doesn't shut up soon.'

'Amber has got a point – about Poppy, anyway,' Abs said. 'She doesn't really *do* anything. At least

The Gems write and sing their own songs.'

'Yeah, but Poppy has all the latest clothes,' Soph said enviously. 'And she's harmless.'

'True,' I agreed. 'But it does seem odd that Amber would say something like that. She didn't come across as the kind of person who would be so mean. Anyway, one thing's for certain. The Gems are getting noticed!'

Chapter Three

I was doing my homework the next night when Abs instant-messaged me.

> **CutiePie**: Hey, check out the *Star Secrets* web site. Amber has said sorry.
> **NosyParker**: You lie!
> **CutiePie**: No, siree.
> **FashionPolice**: And I love, love, love the outfit she wore to say it!!

I had to look. It was true – Amber had made an

apology, saying she liked and respected Poppy. All while wearing a stripy jumper dress. Très chic. But even better, she also said The Gems were playing a gig in London soon – specially for under-eighteens, like us, who couldn't go to some of the swanky clubs they often played in. We HAD to go.

NosyParker: Did you see the gig date? Let's go!

CutiePie: But how? It's in London.

FashionPolice: I'll call Penny. She'll have us to stay.

NosyParker: That would be awesome! :-)

After much pleading and lots of promises, it was all arranged. Penny, Soph's totally cool aunt, was happy to take us to the gig and we were going to stay at her flat afterwards. I love staying there – Penny is really nice and totally relaxed. Unlike some of *my* family members.

'But you'll miss the murder-mystery night I'm hosting,' Nan said.

She and her friend Gerry had decided to organise a murder-mystery party, where everyone had to dress up as various characters and guess who the murderer was. The theme was horse-racing. Mum and her friend Sally were going as jockeys and they'd been discussing their costumes for about two weeks. I didn't think there were that many different outfits a jockey could wear, but there you are. Nan had wanted me to go as a famous horse trainer. She was going to be a bookie, taking people's bets. It would have been the most embarrassing and also boring party ever. I was totally relieved I was going to miss it, but I couldn't say that to Nan.

'You can tell me all about it when I get back,' I said. 'You wouldn't want me there anyway. I'm so good at solving mysteries, I'd guess the murderer before all of you!'

Nan gave me a look. 'I don't think so, dear,' she said.

* * *

Me, Abs and Soph could not WAIT to go to London. The gig was on a Friday night, so we obviously paid lots of attention to every lesson that day at school, and answered every question correctly. NOT. Soph had arrived late that morning, lugging a huge bag behind her.

'What the crusty old grandads have you got in there?' Abs asked.

'I couldn't decide what to wear –' Soph puffed.

'So you've brought your whole wardrobe?' I said, raising my eyebrows.

'Cool! You can style us too!' Abs said.

'Er, no, don't worry,' I chipped in quickly. I was perfectly happy with my T-shirt and jeans. I'd had enough makeovers from Soph in the past to know that what works on her *never* works on me.

Somehow, we made it through the day – even double maths. Of course, it always helps that the fabby Mr Adams teaches maths. If only Mum would behave like a normal person every now and then, he might see beyond the revolting leggings and dismal taste in music and find someone he can truly care about. Knowing my luck though, if any teacher was going to fall for my mother, it would probably be Time Lord. Urgh, I can't believe I even thought about that. Horrendissimo.

We were going by train – Penny was meeting us at the station at the other end. I don't think everyone else in the carriage cared quite as much as Soph about seeing all her different potential outfits for the evening, though. In fact, several old ladies tutted when she put a huge pile of shoes on the seat opposite her. They were obviously taking the SEATS ARE NOT FOR FEET sign very literally. Anyway, at least they didn't end up covered in a mountain of clothes, like me and Abs did.

'Soph, do you think you could come to a decision now?' said a very muffled Abs from under a load of jumpers.

Soph stopped rooting in her bag and looked at the tops I was holding up. 'Oh, OK. That one,' she said, pointing to the white top I had in my right hand. 'With the flares I beaded last week. Now, where did I put them?'

Abs sighed.

As soon as Penny saw us, she laughed at Soph's bag. 'So, looking forward to the gig?' she asked, striding along to the tube station.

'Yeah!' Soph puffed, scuttling behind her as fast as she could with her heavy load.

'Thanks so much for having us, Penny,' Abs said.

'My pleasure!' Penny replied. 'I always have fun with you girls. Now, what's this I hear about you having met The Gems already?'

On the way to her flat, we filled her in on the interview and the gig. There was just time for a quick pizza before we had to go. Penny had the coolest flat ever, and probably the cleanest kitchen too. She was about as good at cooking as my mum – but she hardly ever bothered to cook anyway. Pizza was definitely safer.

'Right then, you three,' Penny said, chucking the empty pizza box in her recycling bin. 'Washing up's done. Let's go!'

We were off to see The Gems!

When we got to the club, there was a really long queue outside. Even though we had tickets, we still had to wait. After half an hour, I was getting très twitchy, because the gig was due to start. Penny went up to the front to check what was going on.

'What's the story, Rory?' I asked when she came back.

'They had to stop the queue while some VIPs arrived,' Penny explained. 'They've just started letting everyone in again. We should be in there soon.'

'I hope so,' Soph muttered. 'This top isn't as warm as it looks.'

'I wonder which VIPs are here,' I said.

'Probably those Z-list ones who go to everything,' Abs said. 'Look at the paparazzi.'

There were loads of blokes with cameras round their necks hanging around and chatting. It must be a weird life, stalking celebs – you spend the whole time standing around in the street, waiting for them to go in or out of a door. Still, if these people didn't do their jobs, we'd have no pics to look at in *Star Secrets*!

We finally got into the club at 7.30, when the gig was due to start. Luckily, The Gems were late coming on stage, so we had time to push through the crowd, getting about halfway to the stage. There was no chance of getting to the front though. It was packed. We were standing off to the side, too, annoyingly. But we could see the stage, which was the main thing. It was really dark, with spotlights picking out three different places on the stage. It was totally atmospheric. And totally about one billion times better than the Fleetwich shopping centre.

When The Gems came on, there was loads of screaming from the crowd. Almost everyone there was a girl. Actually, thinking about it, I guess boys aren't interested in all-girl pop groups – not in their music, anyway. And it was mostly mums who'd come along with their daughters.

The Gems sang all their hits, and even did a cover version of a Mirage Mullins song, which was totally cool. Since we'd helped Mirage out with a problem she was having with her manager, her career had rocketed along. That song had been number one for weeks, so it was pretty brave of The Gems to do a completely funked-up version, rather than the soulful love song we all knew and loved. Still, Mirage would have approved, I reckoned.

'Thanks, London!' Carly yelled at the end. 'You've been great!'

The three of them then did a pirouette – in perfect time! – and walked off the stage. We all clapped and cheered for ages, but they didn't come back for an encore. The lights came on, and we blinked at each other.

'It must take them *ages* to learn those routines,' I said, thinking how long it takes me to learn to do anything in PE, even a star jump.

'They practise every day,' Abs said. 'It says so on their web site. They're totally professional.'

'Hey, look!' Soph said, pointing behind me. 'It's the door backstage!'

'No way, José!' I gasped, spinning round.

She was right! There was a bouncer standing in front of it, looking all serious. A group had already formed round him, begging him to let them in.

'So, do you think we should try to get backstage?' Soph asked.

'Er, do the French like frog-flavoured crisps?' I said, marching towards the door.

'I can't wait to see this!' Penny said, as the others followed me.

'Hello, we've interviewed The Gems before –' I began. But the bouncer cut me off.

'Have you got a pass?' he asked in a bored tone.

'Well, no, but we work for *Star Secrets* – well, I do –'

'No pass, no entry,' he said, moving forwards to shunt us out of the way. As he did so, I caught a glimpse of someone behind him wearing the very outfit The Gems had worn on stage!

'Amber!' I yelled, practically in the bouncer's ear. 'It's me, Rosie!'

It *was* Amber! She came over to the door and everyone went wild. The bouncer was looking very annoyed now and grabbed hold of my arm, trying to get me out of the way.

'Hi, Amber!' I said breathlessly, fighting to get my arm free.

'Great gig!' Soph and Abs chorused, beaming at her.

'Thanks!' she said, tossing her hair back. 'Hey, do you guys want to come backstage?'

'Does Poppy Carlton like shoes?' I said, finally wrestling free of the bouncer, who had been distracted by Soph's insane grin.

Amber looked confused.

'She means yes please!' Abs said quickly.

'Come on then!' Amber said. 'John, can you let these three in?'

'And my Aunt Penny!' Soph said.

'Sure,' Amber said. 'John?'

The bouncer stood aside grumpily. I tried not to grin *too* much as I walked past. Well, OK, I smirked like a loon at him. Behind us, the crowd surged forwards. He'd soon forget us – he was going to be busy!

We followed Amber round a corner and up some stairs. 'We're in here,' she said. 'Grab yourselves a drink. I've just gotta go and change.'

Wow! The place was full of celebs! There was practically the whole cast of my fave soap, plus loads of reality TV stars. I started breathing really fast – it was like my dream come true! Me and loads of celebs! Hobnobbing!

Abs nudged me. 'Look! There's Poppy Carlton.'

Poppy was surrounded by paparazzi (how had *they* got in?), posing and flicking her hair. She totally looked like Amanda Hawkins actually. Oh, no! You *could* have a career just hair-flicking!!

At that moment, we spotted Rach and Carly. They were sitting at a booth in the corner with some other people. Penny recognised one girl.

'Hi, Fleur!' she said, air-kissing her hello. 'How are you doing?'

'Good, thanks!' Fleur said. 'How come you're here?'

'I'm with these three,' Penny said, gesturing at

me, Abs and Soph. We were just standing there, gawping at them. 'Chaperoning, you know. You?'

'Oh, I'm doing make-up for The Gems now,' Fleur said.

'Brilliant! So, how's Dave?' Penny said.

Fleur sighed. Penny put her arm round her and they walked off together, chatting.

'Man trouble,' Abs said knowledgeably.

'Have you got drinks yet?' Amber asked, sliding into the booth, next to Carly. She'd changed into jeans and a T-shirt.

We shook our heads.

'Hi, girls,' said a deep voice behind us. We turned round. It was Mr Smith, Amber's dad. 'You pop up everywhere! You must be The Gems' number-one fans! Although I'd say you've got competition now – they were going crazy for you girls out there.' He laughed heartily and sat down next to Rach, who beamed.

'It was a great concert,' I said. 'And –'

'Julia!' Mr Smith suddenly yelled to a girl walking past. 'Drinks for The Gems! Now!'

Julia nodded and scuttled off.

'Erm,' I said. I'd lost my train of thought. I looked at Amber. She was fiddling with a paper napkin.

'Girls, please sit down,' her dad barked at us. 'You're standing in the way. The cameras want to see The Gems!' He pointed to the paparazzi, who were hovering nearby. Actually, they looked like they were more interested in snapping Poppy than The Gems, but whatever.

We slid into the booth next to Amber, who smiled half-heartedly at me.

'So, you liked the concert?' she asked.

'Yeah! It was brilliant,' I said.

'Your dancing was amazing,' Abs said.

Amber winced. 'Thanks. I'm not so keen on the dancing actually,' she said quietly. 'I think all that co-ordinated stuff is a bit much, you know?'

'No, it's great!' I said. 'You're like the perfect pop group!'

Amber sighed at this, instead of looking pleased. Just then, Julia came up and gave her a drink. She sipped at it as if she didn't really want it.

Rach and Carly, on the other hand, were chatting away to everyone who came up to the booth, and grinning madly. The two of them were soon ordering snacks, air-kissing everyone and posing for pictures. Mr Smith had gone to the bar and was talking to some bloke there, laughing heartily.

I turned to say something to Amber, and saw she'd moved into the corner and was fiddling with her phone. I smiled at her, and she smiled back, but she didn't look like she wanted to talk to anyone.

So me, Abs and Soph sipped our lemonades and celeb-watched for a bit. We sat at the edge of the booth, soaking up the atmosphere. Everyone was so *loud*!

'Come on,' I said. 'Let's mingle!' I mean, hel-lo? We were at a party with loads of celebs. As a part-time *Star Secrets* journalist, it was practically my *duty* to talk to them.

'We can't just go up and talk to people!' hissed Abs. 'What will we say?'

'Look, we'll pretend we're going to the bar. Or the loo,' I said. 'That'll get a conversation going.'

Soph and Abs looked at me. 'Right,' Soph said. 'A conversation about how you need the loo. Thrilling.'

'Well, it's better than sitting here just watching everyone,' I said. 'Look! There's that bloke who's cheating on his wife with her son's girlfriend!' I pointed to a soap actor at the bar.

Abs rolled her eyes. 'Lead on then, Rosie. Lead on,' she said.

I have to say my plan was très bon. Even Soph and Abs admitted it. Pretending we had to get somewhere meant we had to squeeze past all these celebs, which gave us loads of chances to earwig on their convos. Sometimes we managed to talk to them too. Soph got the name of a great second-hand clothes shop for next time she was up in London from a girl-band member, and Abs managed to tell a totally hot actor how good he was in his latest TV drama.

'You mean how gorgey he is,' Soph said,

nudging Abs once the actor had turned to talk to someone else.

'You've gone all red!' I said.

'Sssh!' Abs said, looking embarrassed.

'Hey, shall I ask Poppy Carlton what her next project is?' I said. I was totally feeling brave after all this chatting. 'You know, see if she's actually planning to *do* anything?'

'Oooh, get you,' Abs said.

Just then, Penny found us. 'Sorry, girls,' she said. 'We should go. It's getting late.'

'Zut alors,' I said, gutted.

'Let's just say bye to The Gems,' Soph said.

We went back to The Gems' booth and yelled goodbye at them. Amber smiled at us and waved. Rach and Carly didn't hear us – they were surrounded by people – so we shrugged and headed back to Penny's flat. What a très, très fab evening!

✳ ✳ ✳

That Sunday morning, Mum popped to the shop for the papers and some more biscuits for Nan. Nan goes even more doolally than normal if there aren't at least two packets of biscuits in the house at all times.

'If they don't have any custard creams, don't buy digestives!' she yelled as Mum went out of the door. 'I only buy the digestives in Fleetwich!'

Good grief. Why do I have to listen to this madness instead of being allowed a lie-in like a normal teenager? I groaned and pulled the duvet over my head.

I was just drifting off again into a marvelloso dream about singing live in concert with The Gems when Mum yelled from the hall, 'I've got your magazine, Rosie!'

What magazine?

Star Secrets comes out on Tuesdays. Sacrebleu, it looked like I was going to get no sleep at all. And it was only 11 o'clock!

I rolled out of bed grumpily and trudged downstairs.

'Rosie, look!' Mum said proudly, pointing at a magazine on the kitchen table.

I peered at it. It was *Sunday Stars*, which comes with the paper and which I never read, since *Star Secrets* is *so* much better. But this week it had humongous pictures of Amber and Poppy on the front, with the words 'Poppy Sees Red' splashed over them!

'Cool! Thanks, Mum!' I grabbed it and found the article.

'I knew you'd like it,' Mum said happily as she put the kettle on. 'I thought, ah, there's that girl from that band Rosie likes, and something's obviously happened between her and that other girl, and I know Rosie likes to keep up to date with the latest gossip –'

'Mu-um! I'm trying to read the article!' I said.

'Well, sor-ree,' she said, looking hurt. 'I just thought you'd appreciate the gesture.'

I jumped up and hugged her, feeling guilty. 'Of course I do – sorry. I'm just still really sleepy. I think I'll go and read it in bed. Thanks!'

I went back upstairs and snuggled under the duvet again. Good old Mum. She does chunter on, but she's lovely sometimes.

Now I could actually concentrate on the magazine, I learned Poppy had said some evil things about Amber. Which was totally weird. I mean, I knew they had pretty much ignored each other after the gig, and Amber had apologised for her comments ages ago.

I got out my phone and texted Abs and Soph.

Me: Poppy was mean about Amber!

Abs: R U serious? Y?

Me: Dunno. Jealous??

Soph: But she has all the best stuff!

Me: Yeah, but A has talent.

Abs: But A said soz.

Me: I know! Très odd.

Something was going on in the land of celebs. Either Poppy and Amanda Hawkins were practically identical twins – the hair-tossing and witchiness matched, anyway – or someone was a Garibaldi short of a biscuit tin. Poppy had never seemed the nasty type, though. Ditzy, yes, but not nasty. And Amber had been so nice when we'd first met her. Something didn't quite add up.

Chapter Four

About a week after Poppy shockingly lashed out at Amber, I got a call after school.

'Hello, could I speak to Rosie Parker please?' said a voice.

'This is she. I mean, her. I mean, I'm Rosie Parker,' I said.

'Hi, Rosie! It's Judy!' the person cried.

Judy? Who was Judy?

'Hi, Judy!' I replied, hoping I sounded like I recognised her voice.

'I was wondering if you and your friends

wanted to come for a ride on Saturday?'

A *ride*? Had we recently met someone who had horses? Had I totally forgotten? Was I going mad?

'Erm . . .' I said. I wasn't *desperate* to get on a horse, if I'm honest. Although many celebs do recommend it for toning the stomach and thighs.

'It's not as bad as rush hour during the week, but the traffic's still pretty busy in town on a Saturday afternoon,' Judy continued. 'I thought you might like to do a mini-report.'

Oh! It was the traffic-helicopter lady! Cool!

'Oh, yes!' I said. 'Brilliant. Great. Totally.'

'I'll expect you at the station at about two o'clock then?' Judy said.

'We'll be there!' I said.

Soph and Abs were totally up for it when I told them. Except it meant more time away from Dream Beauty for Soph.

'I can't wait to see the traffic jams and how long they are,' Abs said.

No, she didn't really. But we did agree it would be pretty cool to spot our houses from the air. Even boring Borehurst must look more interesting from that angle.

Mum drove us to the radio station again. This time I'd grabbed The Gems' album first and quickly shoved it in the CD player, so she couldn't sing along to any of her golden oldies. Instead, we sang along to The Gems. Well, Abs and I did. Soph did what she *thinks* is singing, but is actually hitting all the wrong notes at the wrong time and in the wrong order. Even Mum was wincing.

Judy was waiting in reception for us. We waved goodbye to Mum as Judy bundled us into a van to go to the airfield. It was so exciting!

'The weather is perfect today,' Judy said. 'Not too cloudy and no rain. We'll be able to see a lot.'

'And are we going to fly over Borehurst as well as Fleetwich?' I asked. 'I want to wave to my nan!'

Great, Rosie. Way to sound about five years old.

Judy laughed. 'Yup. We'll be covering an area of twenty square miles in total. So we'll probably fly over your houses.'

'Megan is sooo jealous,' Abs said as we pulled

up at the airfield. 'She's going to be waiting in the garden to see us.' Megan is Abs's five-year-old sister. She normally doesn't think we're very cool, because we're not interested in playing princesses. But today going in a helicopter made us interesting.

We got out of the van and Judy took us to meet the pilot.

'Hi, girls! Glad to have you aboard. I'm Mike,' he said, shaking our hands. 'It's going to be cosy in there today.' He gestured at the ginormous helicopter behind him. I gulped. Were we really going to go up in the air in *that*?

'Ready?' Judy asked.

We all nodded.

She and Mike got in the front seats and the three of us squished in the seats behind them and strapped ourselves in tightly. We each had a pair of headphones to put on.

'They block out the noise,' Judy said. 'We'll need them once the rotors get going. But you can talk to us and each other through these microphones here.' She pointed to the Madonnastyle mike attached to the headphones as she put them on.

We put ours on. I was by the left window, next to Soph, and Abs had the right window.

'Ready, girls?' Mike asked.

We grinned at him.

'Here we go!' He pressed a few buttons and suddenly the helicopter was filled with noise. Really loud noise.

I looked out of the window and saw the blades starting to whip round. They went faster and faster until they were a blur. Soph grabbed my hand as the whole machine began juddering. Then we slowly rose up from the ground.

I glanced across at Abs. She had a look of concentration on her face. She was probably working out the speed of the rotor blades versus the velocity of the engine or something. Her genius brain never rests.

Judy turned round and gave us the thumbs-up. 'We're going to Borehurst first, girls,' she said over the intercom. 'Watch out for jams!'

Five useful things NOT to do when in a traffic helicopter and live on air:

1. Try to lean out and wave at your mum – you'll only bash your head on the window.
2. Say, 'Look at that humongous traffic jam – it'll take ages to get through that!'
3. Take your earphones off. It's REALLY loud!
4. Pretend you're a celeb in a private helicopter and order your mates about like they're your servants.
5. Keep saying, 'Should it be that loud? What's that noise? How are we staying in the air again?' You'll freak EVERYONE out!

It was really cool to watch as we went back the way we'd come, but in the air. It took about five minutes, not half an hour. If only we could travel by helicopter every day. Imagine turning up to school like that, landing on the netball court and watching Amanda Hawkins's face as we sauntered out like celebs. She would be green with envy!

I wished she could see us now.

Soph leaned across me. 'Look!' she shrieked. 'It's my house!'

Abs leaned over to our side too. 'Where? Where?'

'Oh, it's gone now,' Soph said. 'My garden looked so small!'

We must have been pretty high up, cos Soph's garden is massive.

'Over there, Mike,' Judy said suddenly. 'Looks pretty chocka.'

We swung round to the right and hovered over the entrance to the huge supermarket on the road to Fleetwich. It was packed with cars. Obviously everyone was doing their shopping at the same time. Maybe there was a special offer on biscuits or something.

'I'll record this, I think, Mike,' Judy said.

Mike nodded and made the helicopter swoop round again.

Judy patched in to the radio station and waited for her cue from the DJ. 'This is Judy Baker reporting from the Fleetwich FM traffic helicopter at midday,' she said. 'If you're planning on doing your weekly shop, why not wait an hour or so. There are currently long queues right up to the slip road.'

Judy pressed a few buttons and then gave us the thumbs-up again. Obviously, we were supposed to be thrilled by this part of her job. We all replied with the thumbs-up too. Although, *personally*, I'm still going to be a celeb journalist. Traffic reporting just doesn't quite cut it for me.

We circled once more, and then sped off over Borehurst again. I was beginning to recognise the town from the air. I could see our school, and the town centre. That building with the car park behind it must be Trotters – Nan's fave café.

'There's the beauty salon!' Soph suddenly shrieked, stretching across me to point out of the window again. She was 'sick' today, so it was lucky we were miles in the air and her boss couldn't hear her screeching.

We were just getting close to where my house is

when the helicopter suddenly whirled away in the other direction.

'Looks hectic over here,' Judy said. 'Right, girls, it's your turn. All you need to say is, "We're in the Fleetwich FM traffic helicopter at midday. There are tailbacks of half a mile on the Fleetwich to Bichester road. Take alternative routes where possible." OK? You can do a sentence each.'

'OK,' we all said.

'I'll go first,' Soph said, like she knew what she was doing.

'OK, then you, Rosie, then Abs,' Judy said. She pressed a button, waited for the DJ to cue us in, and pointed at Soph.

'We're in the Fleetwich FM traffic helicopter at midday,' Soph said.

Judy pointed at me.

'Er, there are tailbacks of half a mile on the Fleetchester to Biwich road. Oh, no, I mean, the Fleetwich and Bichester road,' I said, all flustered. Talk about cringe-tastic!

Abs rolled her eyes. 'Take alternative routes

where possible,' she said smoothly.

Why oh why am I always the one to make a fool of myself?

* * *

After twenty minutes of circling about and Judy doing more reports, we headed back. I was keeping pretty quiet – I had made a total idiot of myself, after all. Even though the stuff Judy had to report on wasn't fascinating, it was pretty cool flying about in a helicopter. And she got to do it every day! How awesome was that?

As we flew slowly back over Fleetwich, I saw a long pink car draw up to a house and a blonde girl get out. We were pretty low down by then, so she looked up to see what was making the noise and I caught sight of her face for a second. It was Poppy Carlton! I gasped and nudged Soph.

'What?' she said, leaning across.

'It's Poppy Carlton!' I said.

'Really?' everyone said, peering down. 'Where?'

'There! Just going up to that house.'

'Rosie, are you seeing things again?' Abs asked.

'No, honestly, it was her. Quick, let's remember where it is.' I pressed my face against the glass and stared down as we moved further and further away. 'There's a park a few houses away, and a roundabout up the hill. That's all I can see.'

We were too far away now to see anything else. I sat back in my seat to find Soph and Abs staring at me. 'What?' I said. 'It was her! She looked up at the helicopter and she had the same hair and everything.'

'Well, what is she doing in Fleetwich?' Abs asked sensibly.

'I don't know, do I?' I said. Hmm, come to think of it, I was sure I'd read about her latest holiday in *Star Secrets* that week. She'd been in the Caribbean. 'She must be back from her hols.'

'Right. And she'd rush straight from the Caribbean to Fleetwich, of course,' Abs said sarcastically.

'Quite a few famous people live in Fleetwich,

actually,' Judy butted in. 'There's that bloke off the telly with the puppet. Oh, what's his name? You know.'

We pretended to look interested, but my brain was whirring. What was Poppy doing in Fleetwich?

Just then, the airfield came into view. I could see a small figure waving madly as we approached. A small figure wearing green leggings. Oh, no, it was my mum. The shame! I had to get us out of there and quickly, or she'd try to get herself and the Banana Splits on the radio.

We landed and Mike turned the engine off. Slowly, the noise died down and the blades stopped rotating. We took our headphones off.

'Thanks so much,' Abs said. 'We had a great time.'

'Yes, thanks!' Soph said. 'It was so cool to see my house!'

'Our pleasure,' Judy said. 'Thanks for helping with the report!'

I flushed with shame at the memory. 'Right, well, there's my mum. We'd better get going,' I gabbled, scrambling out of the helicopter. 'Thanks again!'

Mum was striding towards us. 'I heard you on the radio!' she was saying. 'My little girl!' Sacrebleu! As if I hadn't embarrassed myself enough for one day!

'Excellent. Right, come on, Mum. We have to get back now, don't we?' I said, taking her arm and swinging her back in the direction of the car. 'Come on, Abs, Soph.'

They trotted after us and we all got into the car.

'So, was it exciting to be up in the sky?' Mum asked.

'Yeah, it was actually,' I said, buckling myself in. 'And guess who I saw? Poppy Carlton!'

'Well, you saw someone who *looked* like Poppy Carlton,' Abs said.

'What was she wearing?' Soph asked.

'I dunno. A green jacket, I think. I only saw her briefly,' I replied. 'But I know it was her!'

'Well, let's go and see where she was going then,' Abs suggested.

'Good thinking, Batgirl. Mum,' I said, turning and smiling sweetly at the be-legginged one. 'Could we go back through Fleetwich please? We want to see what it looks like from the ground this time.'

Mum glanced at me. 'You know what Fleetwich looks like from the ground. You're always complaining about how boring it is,' she said.

Great.

Luckily, Abs had a plan. 'But we saw there was a large build-up of traffic on the ringroad to Borehurst,' she said. 'It'd probably be quicker going through the town.'

'OK then,' said Mum, sighing. 'Since you're such experts on the roads now, you can direct me.'

Excellent! Now we had to find the park, and a roundabout . . .

Ten minutes later, we'd found them, and we made Mum go slowly down the road.

'I'm pretty sure it was this one,' I muttered.

'There's no pink car here now,' Soph said.

'Ooh, but I recognise that big tree,' I said.

'It's outside The Gems' house!' Abs said.

I looked again. She was right! There'd been a feature on it in *Star Secrets* a few weeks ago. The band had done an 'at home' feature and talked about living together and who did the washing-up and all that stuff. They'd posed for loads of photos in their lounge, and there'd been one small shot of the front of the house. Not so you'd know where it was, but you could definitely see the same massive tree in the front drive.

'Slow down, Mum!' I said. 'This is where The Gems live!'

Mum rolled her eyes, but slowed the car down to a crawl.

'So, it was one of The Gems you saw then?' Soph asked, as we all gaped at the house.

'No, I'm sure it was Poppy,' I insisted. 'The Gems don't have a pink car, anyway.'

'But why would Poppy visit them?' Soph wondered.

'Maybe to sort out the feud between her and Amber?' Abs suggested.

'Yeah,' I said slowly. 'Maybe.'

There was something very odd about the whole thing.

* * *

A few days later, Abs grabbed me at break. 'Look,' she said, pointing at a mag. 'Poppy's still in the Caribbean.'

I looked at the photos of a very tanned Poppy in a teeny tiny bikini on the beach.

'So it can't have been her you saw on Saturday,' Soph said, helpfully.

'I guess not,' I said. 'It looked so like her, though. I wonder who it was?'

Abs rolled her eyes. 'It could have been anyone!' she said. 'Amber's blonde – it could have been a relative of hers.'

'Or a friend,' Soph said.

'Yes, but there was something Poppy-ish about her,' I began.

'Look, Rosie. We all know you can usually spot

a celeb like Soph can spot a fashion error, but this time you're wrong,' Abs said. 'It can't have been Poppy. End of story.'

I sighed. I'd been so sure. But maybe Abs and Soph were right. It couldn't have been her. It was a mystery person. And it looked like we weren't going to find out who this mystery person was.

Chapter Five

For the next few weeks, all the papers and mags could talk about was the feud between Poppy and Amber. There were loads of pictures of Poppy, posing like her life depended on it, and interviews where she said things like, 'I thought Amber was really nice when I first met her. But she's actually really horrible!'

Amber was usually reported as saying 'No comment', and in interviews with Rach and Carly, she would be as nice as pie and just talk about the band. But then the next day the papers would claim she'd said something about Poppy having no talent again. She seemed to swing back and forth between being nice and being nasty. Très bizarro.

'I wonder if the other girls are annoyed Amber's getting all the headlines?' Abs said one day. We were in her room, idly scrolling through a gossip web site, and there were loads more photos of Amber than Rach and Carly.

'Probably,' Soph said. 'It's weird how she's suddenly gone all mouthy and nasty. She seemed really normal when we met her.'

'That's fame for you,' I sighed. 'It changes everyone.'

'Yeah, but so quickly?' Abs said. 'The three of them were supposed to be really close, but now you mostly see just Rach and Carly, or Amber by herself.'

'Well, maybe she's sick of them,' I suggested. 'Knowing them for years, putting up with all their quirks, seeing them every day. I know how she feels . . .'

'Hey!' Soph and Abs said.

'Only joking, mes amis,' I said. 'I agree, actually. It's très odd how they are all co-ordinated and stuff when performing or in interviews together, and Amber seems so nice and normal, and then bam! Suddenly, she comes out with another classic insult for Poppy.'

'Yeah, and why Poppy in particular?' Abs said. 'What's she got against her?'

'Maybe the papers are making it all up,' Soph said.

'*Star Secrets* is very professional,' I said indignantly. 'They would never make stuff up.'

'Well, something's really weird. It's like Amber is two different people,' Abs said.

I gasped suddenly. 'Maybe she's got an evil twin!'

Soph and Abs laughed. 'Hel-*lo*? Someone's been watching too many murder mysteries!' Abs said.

I had to admit it was a bit far-fetched. Even Nan wouldn't really believe that. 'OK, maybe not,' I said. 'But at least that would explain it!'

I jiggled my legs with frustration. It was a real mystery. And I didn't know how to solve it!

* * *

About three weeks after we'd gone up in the helicopter, I trailed home from school. I'd had a tough day. Amanda Witchface had been particularly evil in PE, and Mr Adams was so chirpy, I just knew he'd fallen in love with someone and my (admittedly slow-to-get-going) plan to get him to ask Mum out was ruined before it even started.

I sighed heavily as I closed the front door.

'Is that you, Rosie?' Mum called. 'We're up here!'

It sounded suspiciously like her voice came from my room. I bounded up the stairs to find that, yes, Mum and Nan were making themselves comfortable at the computer. Good grief. Did the word 'privacy' mean nothing to them?

'Hello, dear,' Nan said. 'Come and look at this.

I'm going to be Jessica Fletcher!'

What the crusty old grandads was she going on about? I hoped it wasn't another murder-mystery party – they'd had such a good time at the last one, I knew they'd want to do it again. I started to work out excuses for not being there.

'Me and your nan have decided we should do a bit of extra work to save up for our next holiday,' Mum said, clicking on something that opened a new web page.

I peered over her shoulder.

'We thought we could be lookalikes!' Mum continued, scrolling down through a load of pictures of celebs. 'I can be Keren from Bananarama –'

'And I can be Jessica Fletcher!' Nan trilled, all excited.

No way, José! Just when I think they've done all they can to embarrass me, they come up with new forms of torture.

'Right,' I said weakly. 'Great.'

'It's very well paid,' Mum said excitedly. 'Look, here's someone who looks like that rugby player, whatever his name is. They can earn two hundred pounds per appearance!'

I didn't point out it was unlikely there would be quite as much demand for an eighties pop singer and a granny who solved crimes. I value my life, after all.

Mum carried on scrolling through the pictures. There were loads of 'celebs' on the books – footballers, singers, TV personalities . . . even Poppy Carlton!

'The agency's based in Fleetwich,' Mum was saying as I stared at the picture of 'Poppy'. 'So I could head there after work one day and see if they're interested.'

Fleetwich. There was a lookalike agency with a 'Poppy' on their books in Fleetwich! That would explain it! I *knew* I wasn't seeing things! I had to tell Abs and Soph.

'Brilliant, Mum!' I said. 'Why don't you call them now? Look, there's their phone number. Sorry to kick you out, but I really have to do my homework.'

'Good idea,' Mum said, getting up.

'Remember to ask the agency about me too,' Nan said, following her out.

I shut the door behind them and immediately texted Abs and Soph:

> **Me:** Get online now! I was right!
> **Abs:** ??
> **Me:** About Poppy.
> **Soph:** What r u on about?
> **Me:** Tell u online.

While I waited for them to sign in, I looked at the picture of 'Poppy' again. It was spooky – she looked exactly like the real thing!

> **CutiePie:** OK, so what are you right about this time?
> **NosyParker:** I did see Poppy from the helicopter. Well, her lookalike anyway.
> **FashionPolice:** Yes, we know you saw someone who looked like Poppy. Big deal.

NosyParker: No! I mean someone who is her professional lookalike! Check out an agency called Reflections. It's in Fleetwich!

CutiePie: So you think it wasn't the real Poppy, but the fake one?

NosyParker: Bien sûr, ma soeur. The question is: why would the fake Poppy go to The Gems' house?

FashionPolice: To stir up trouble?

CutiePie: To get tips on singing?

NosyParker: I dunno. But I reckon if we could talk to her, we could find out.

Chapter Six

'Right, so you know what you're saying?' I asked Abs the next day after school. We were sitting in front of my computer, the Reflections site flashing at us.

Abs nodded. 'Why do *I* have to call, though?'

Soph sighed. 'We've told you. You've got the best grown-up voice on the phone, Abs. Remember that time I thought you were your mum?'

Abs giggled at the memory. 'You were so polite!' she said.

Oh, for the love of flip-flops. 'Come on!' I urged. 'Just call them!'

'OK, OK,' Abs said. 'Keep your hair on.' She dialled the agency's number. 'Hello? Ah, hello. I'd like to book one of your lookalikes, please . . . yes, Poppy Carlton . . . It's Melanie Walker from Modo in the Borehurst shopping mall. We're opening a new store in a few days' time and we'd love Poppy to come and officially launch it! . . . Uh-huh . . . Yes.' Abs started making panicked faces at us. 'Er, well, I can't send you an email to confirm this, I'm afraid. The builders are still in there and we have no electricity . . . I *know*, they tell you it'll take two weeks and it takes four! . . . Lovely, yes, thank you.'

Abs grinned at us. 'They've just gone to get the diary,' she whispered. Me and Soph gave her the thumbs-up. 'Hello? Yes, Poppy Carlton . . . Um, no, I don't think we'll be wanting him as well, thank you . . . Well, that's an excellent deal, but he's not really the sort of celebrity our target customer wants to meet . . . I know – he reads the news very well. But we'll just have Poppy, thank you . . . Great! We'd need her at about one o'clock on Saturday . . . Fantastic! Thank you so much. Goodbye!'

Soph and I were seriously impressed.

'You are a genius, Abigail Flynn,' I said. 'Totally convincing.'

'Yup,' Soph agreed. 'I'm really looking forward to looking at Modo's stuff, too!'

We looked at her. 'Soph, that's the bit we made up,' Abs said. 'You know. Cos it's Poppy's favourite shop. To get the fake Poppy to come over.'

'Oh, yeah.' Soph looked gutted. 'Oh, well.'

'The main thing is, we'll be there to talk to her,' I said. 'And to find out how come she went to The Gems' house that time, when the real Poppy and Amber are supposed to be having this feud.'

'Right,' said Soph. 'I wonder what she'll wear.'

Abs and I both hit her with pillows.

✳ ✳ ✳

That Saturday, Abs and I met Soph outside Dream Beauty. She'd managed to finish her shift at lunchtime.

'I hope "Poppy" turns up,' I said.

'She will,' Abs said confidently. 'The woman totally bought my story.'

We got to the mall just before one, so positioned ourselves in the café with some smoothies. There was a shop opposite called Mode, and we guessed 'Poppy' might think it was the shop she was supposed to be opening.

'Look, there she is!' I squeaked as a tall, slim, blonde girl walked up to the shop and paused outside. She went in and talked to the shop assistant for a few minutes.

'She doesn't look happy,' Abs whispered.

The fake Poppy was waving her arms about now as she argued with the shop assistant, who kept shrugging. Finally, she stomped out of the shop and went over to the map of the mall, by the escalators. Obviously, she couldn't find Modo on the list.

'We've got to talk to her!' I hissed.

'She's coming this way!' Soph said, then she slurped her smoothie really noisily. I really wanted to laugh.

'Poppy' spotted the café and came in. She ordered a coffee and started rummaging in her handbag.

'She's got a Sanauri bag!' said Soph excitedly.

'A what?' I said. Honestly, Soph has a one-track mind.

'It's the latest must-have bag,' Soph explained.

'Right,' I said, watching 'Poppy' as she tried to juggle her coffee and with her mobile.

She sat down near us and began arguing into her phone. 'But that's what I said! They said they hadn't called you. And they're called Mode, anyway, not Modo . . . There must have been some mix-up . . . Well, I'm definitely here, and there's no shop-opening . . . Fine.' She snapped her phone shut angrily.

Me, Soph and Abs looked at each other. Oops. That was our fault. Still, we had to talk to her or it was a complete waste of time.

Soph suddenly got up and sat down at the table next to 'Poppy'. 'Has anyone ever told you that you look *exactly* like Poppy Carlton?' she said.

'Poppy' turned to her, sighing. 'Yes, they have. In fact, I'm her lookalike.'

'*Are* you?' Soph said, sounding really impressed. 'Wow! I love your handbag, by the way,' she said. 'Is it a Sanauri?'

'Poppy' relaxed and grinned at her. 'Yes it is. I got it off eBay.'

'Oh, I love it! I so want one,' Soph said. 'It's much more practical than those small bags that were all the rage last season.' 'Poppy' was nodding. 'And when you wear them with skinny jeans they make you look even smaller than you are!'

'I know!' 'Poppy' said. 'I just hope they'll stay in fashion for a while. I can't afford to keep getting new bags.'

'Yeah,' Soph nodded. 'But you can always customise stuff to look different. And it's good to look like you're ahead of the game rather than following everyone else, anyway.'

Me and Abs moved closer now. Soph was good! 'Poppy' was totally eating out of her hand!

'Unfortunately, I have to stick with whatever

Poppy does, though,' 'Poppy' said. She laughed wryly. 'I even have to wear contact lenses instead of my glasses when I'm on a job, which is expensive.'

'You must be getting booked quite a lot at the moment though,' Abs said.

'Yeah. I thought I'd been booked today, but it turns out there's been some mix-up. I don't know what happened, but it's really annoying, because I'm not going to get paid and I need the money.'

I gulped. *Guilt! Guilt!*

'Oh, no!' Soph said feebly.

'Yeah, I'm at college. This is just something I do to pay the bills. I guess I'm lucky that I look like someone who's in the papers a lot. I just hope she stays popular for a while longer so I can finish college,' 'Poppy' sighed.

'So you're quite busy at the moment, then?' I pressed.

'Yup. Poppy is definitely in demand. I get quite a few jobs.'

'What kind ? I mean, who books you?' I asked.

'Oh, you know, supermarkets, magazines – that

kind of thing. I've got one client in particular who's been giving me loads of work recently. That's why I could afford this bag!'

'Oh, really? Which client's that?' I asked innocently.

She looked at me sharply. 'Just someone,' she said. 'Anyway, I'd better get back. Since I'm not opening this shop after all, I'd better finish my essay.' She picked up her coffee and her bag. 'Bye! Nice to meet you all!'

'Bye!' we chorused as she left.

'Zut alors!' I said. 'We're no nearer to finding out why she went to see The Gems.'

'And I feel really bad for wasting her time today,' Abs groaned.

'I know,' I said. 'But still, she's had loads of work recently, from someone in particular. I wonder who?'

Soph looked at her watch. 'I'm peckish,' she said. 'Has your nan got any good biscuits in?'

I looked at her. 'Does Time Lord think he's a good actor?'

'Let's go to your house then, Rosie, and work it all out there,' Abs said.

We agreed this was the best plan, so trailed back to the house of madness which I call home. Luckily, neither Mum nor Nan was in, so we raided the biscuit tin and sat in my room, pondering the situation.

'OK, so what do we know so far?' Abs said. 'Let's write it all down.'

Ooh, she's so sensible. I grabbed my notebook and started scribbling:

Six things we know about Poppy and The Gems:

1. The Gems and Poppy have been going to all the same parties and premieres and events recently.
2. Amber says Poppy is famous for doing nothing (true) and causes a massive rumpus.
3. Amber apologises.
4. Poppy says Amber is a witch, for no apparent

reason. The feud continues in the papers with them slagging each other off.

5. The lookalike Poppy is seen (by Rosie) going to The Gems' house while the real Poppy is on holiday.

6. The fake Poppy says one client is giving her loads of work.

'That's it,' I said.

'OK, so maybe someone is hiring the fake Poppy to stir up trouble,' Abs said slowly.

'Yeah, cos the papers would listen to what she said,' Soph said. 'She does look very like the real Poppy.'

Thank you! That's what I said all along. 'And The Gems and Poppy are hot news at the moment,' I said. 'So the papers are going to want to print stuff they say about each other.'

'But *we* know that Amber isn't that nasty in real life,' Abs said.

'Yeah, so how come she looks so mean in the papers?' Soph said.

'Unless someone's making it all up?' I suggested.

'Or someone wants to stir up trouble for Amber, so they make it look like the feud between her and Poppy is still going on,' Abs said.

I had a sudden thought. 'I think there's something going on between Amber and the others. They're definitely not as good friends as they make out.'

'Perhaps it's Rach and Carly then?' Abs suggested.

'Why would they make trouble for Amber?' Soph asked.

'To get her chucked out of the band, maybe?' I said.

'D'you think?' Abs said.

'I don't know. But I think we should tell Amber what we suspect. After all, if you two were stabbing me in the back, I'd want to know!' I said.

'As if. We'd never do that,' Abs said.

'Only if you had something I really wanted. Like a Sanauri bag,' Soph said.

I looked horrified.

'Only joking!' she said. 'Honestly, you're so gullible.'

Soph is really unnerving sometimes.

'So, what's the plan, Stan?' Abs asked.

'Let's go and tell Amber,' I said.

Chapter Seven

Mum had a Banana Splits rehearsal, so she wasn't going to be back for a while, and Nan was visiting Gerry. This was good because they wouldn't ask us where we were going, but bad because we had to get the bus to Fleetwich. It took AGES, and we'd almost talked ourselves out of mentioning anything to Amber, but then we got to the end of their road.

'Right,' I said. 'Let's hope she's in!'

We marched up the drive and knocked on the door. After a few seconds, it opened, and there was Amber!

'Oh, hi, Amber!' I said.

She looked a bit startled, but smiled faintly at us. Her eyes looked a bit puffy, as if she'd been crying. She had her coat on.

'I know it's a bit weird, us turning up like this,' Abs began.

'We want to tell you what we think has been going on,' I said. 'You know –'

Just then, Amber's dad appeared behind her. 'Who is it?' he asked. Then he caught sight of us standing on the doorstep. 'Oh, it's you lot. We haven't got time to talk to fans now. Come on, Amber, we'll be late.'

'Um,' Amber said, looking at us.

Her dad grabbed her arm. 'Amber,' he said warningly. 'The others are waiting. We've got to go.' He pushed her out of the door so me, Abs and Soph had to skip out of the way.

'We're going to talk to the record label,' Amber said to me, looking a bit desperate.

'Just you?' I asked.

Her dad turned from locking the front door.

'Rachel and Carly are already there, and if someone here doesn't get a move on, we'll have wasted everyone's time. And time is money, Amber. If I've told you that once, I've told you a thousand times. Now, COME ON!'

He took her arm again and walked her towards the road. Amber looked back at us, and then stumbled. As she put out a hand to steady herself, her handbag slid off her arm and fell to the ground. Everything fell out of it.

'*Amber!*' her dad said crossly.

We rushed to help her pick everything up.

Amber crouched next to her stuff, sniffing, while her dad sighed heavily.

'Hurry up, Amber! You're so clumsy!' he barked.

'Here you go,' I said, handing her some keys.

'Thanks,' she muttered, staring at the ground.

Soph had gathered up a pair of sunglasses and a notebook and gave them to Amber. When she looked up to take them, I could see her eyes were filling with tears. Poor Amber! I opened my mouth to say something, but her dad cut in.

'Amber! Come on! We need to go *now*,' he shouted, turning towards the car.

She jammed her stuff back in her bag.

'Are you OK?' I asked.

She nodded quickly, stood up, wiped her eyes and put her sunglasses on. 'We've been booked to play at Borehurst Hospital next week,' she said quickly. 'Good for our profile, Dad says.' She sniffed. 'I'd love to see you there.'

'Amber!' her dad barked again. He was in the car now and had started the engine.

She trotted towards the car.

'See you then!' I shouted after her.

She got into the car, and her dad pulled away almost immediately.

Me, Abs and Soph looked at each other.

'What a dragon her dad is!' Abs said.

'Yeah, it's like the band means more to him than his daughter,' I said.

'She looked like she'd been crying,' Soph said.

'And we never got to tell her our theory,' Abs said.

'No. But there's definitely something going on.

She's so unhappy. This Poppy thing can't help,' I said.

We were still standing in The Gems' driveway.

'Hey!' Soph suddenly said. 'What's that?' She bent down and picked something up from the gutter. It was a bit of card.

'Probably fell out of Amber's bag,' I said.

Soph's mouth dropped open.

'What?' Abs said.

Soph turned the card round so we could see what was written on it. Me and Abs gasped.

It said, 'REFLECTIONS'.

'That's the name of the lookalike agency!' I gasped.

'No kidding!' Abs said. 'How come Amber had it in her bag?'

'No idea,' I said. 'This whole thing gets more and more mysterious.'

'Let's go back to yours and work it out,' Abs said.

All the way back on the bus, we went over and over what had happened, but we couldn't make sense of it. My head was starting to hurt.

Nan was in when we got home. 'Hello, girls,' she said. 'Would anyone like a cup of tea and some custard creams?'

'Ooh, that would be lovely,' Abs said, sitting down at the kitchen table and pressing her hands to her forehead. 'We need brain food.'

'Why's that, dear?' Nan asked.

I looked at Abs and Soph. I was thinking it might be worth our while telling Nan. She'd been helpful when we'd solved mysteries before.

'Well,' I said. I took a deep breath, and told her all we knew.

'So, let me get this straight. Amber is being nasty to this Poppy in the papers,' Nan said.

'Yup,' I nodded.

'And Poppy is being nasty back.'

'Yes.'

'And there's also a lookalike Poppy,' Nan said.

'Yes, and we thought Rach and Carly were hiring her, but then Amber had the agency card in her bag!' Abs said.

'So we're confused,' Soph added helpfully.

'Well, it sounds very simple to me,' Nan said calmly, opening another packet of biscuits. 'There was something like it on *Midsomer Murders* the other day. One girl must be jealous of the other girl and she's using the papers to stir up trouble. You should talk to Amber about it. You said she was nice to you.'

'Yeah, but how?' I said. 'We can't just pop round to their house again – her dad is seriously scary!'

'Didn't you say she mentioned something about the hospital?' Nan asked.

'Yes, they're playing a gig there next week,' Abs said. 'We should go. See if we can talk to Amber and find out what she's got to do with Reflections.'

'It sounded like she wanted us to go,' Soph pointed out.

I pulled apart a custard cream thoughtfully. She *had* looked a bit desperate. I began licking the custard-cream bit off one of the halves of the biscuit. Maybe she needed our help. Maybe she'd found the card somewhere and didn't know what to do. By turning up, we were going to be the answer to her problems. And she'd be eternally grateful because she'd only get good publicity from now on and she'd always mention us in interviews and . . .

'Um, Rosie?' Abs said.

I looked up.

'Could you *be* any more disgusting?' she asked, looking at the mess of biscuit in my hand.

Nan tutted. 'You have no respect for the biscuit, Rosie, none at all.'

Sacrebleu. I knew the moment of sanity was too good to last.

Chapter Eight

All that week, I kept hearing the word 'lookalike' – it was starting to drive me mad. Mum had rung Reflections, and was pretty upset when they told her they didn't think there'd be much work for a member of Bananarama.

'I'm sending them my picture anyway,' she said, licking an envelope one evening. 'And my demo CD. That'll convince them. People always want to hire quality.'

Er, yes, Mum. That's why they won't be hiring you.

'Mmm,' I said, trying to escape up to my room.

'And can you believe they weren't interested in a lookalike of Jessica Fletcher either?' Nan chimed in, outraged. 'Although they did say Miss Marple might do better. But I don't know . . .'

'Nan, what's wrong with Miss Marple?'

'I'm not *that* old!' she said.

I rolled my eyes. Honestly, I live in a madhouse.

Even at school, the word 'lookalike' was all around me, like some kind of echo.

'Rosie Parker!' Miss Bertillon said. 'You look like you haven't heard a word I just said!'

'She looks like a dork,' Amanda Hawkins sniggered under her breath.

I ignored her.

'I just can't work out this Amber and Poppy thing,' I said to Soph and Abs at break.

'We'll talk to The Gems at the hospital,' Abs said comfortingly.

But would Amber's dad let us?

* * *

That day, the hospital was packed. The Gems were performing in the gardens, by the children's ward. It was lucky we got there early, because there wasn't room for loads of members of the public. It was a lovely sunny day, and several kids had been wheeled outside in wheelchairs and beds. They looked really excited.

Me, Soph and Abs hovered near the back, by the paparazzi. There were quite a few photographers there – Amber's dad was right when he said it would be good publicity.

'Wonder if Amber will mention Poppy Carlton?' I heard one bloke say to his mate.

'Hope so. My editor wants more dirt on them,' the other guy replied.

'It's a charity gig though,' someone else said. 'They'll just sing the songs, talk to a few sick kids and scarper. There'll be no banter, I bet you.'

'Never say never,' the first bloke said hopefully.

A small stage had been set up for The Gems at one end of the gardens, and they arrived on time, waving cheerily. They were in matching dresses again – all green – and Rach grabbed a mike.

'Hello, Borehurst, we're The Gems!' she said.

The crowd cheered, and the photographers started snapping away.

'It's great to be here, to raise money for the hospital,' she said. 'Here's our latest single: "Crystal Clear".'

They launched into the song, singing live to a backing track, but they couldn't do their normal dance routine because the stage was too small. Me, Soph and Abs were doing it though. Well, we were trying to, but I kept going the wrong way and crashing into them.

'Sorry!' I said for the nine thousandth time.

The Gems were totally awesome. They were really good at talking to the crowd and getting them to clap and sing along. They looked très happy up there, even Amber. I wondered if it was because she didn't have to do the dance routine.

When they'd sung all their songs, they thanked the hospital for letting them perform, and disappeared.

'We have to find them!' I said, pushing through the crowd towards the stage. 'Come on!'

Abs and Soph followed me as I elbowed my way through.

The Gems had gone into a small tent at the side of the stage, but there was a bouncer at the roped entrance, and he wasn't letting anyone in.

'But we know them!' I pleaded.

'We've got a message for Amber,' Abs said.

'Yeah, so has everybody. Look, girls, you can't come in,' the bouncer said.

I could see The Gems behind him, and tried to catch Amber's eye, but she looked away.

'Amber!' I called.

I could see Amber's dad next to her. He turned to look in my direction and frowned. Amber was staring at the ground.

'Please leave now,' the bouncer said, putting his arm in front of me.

After ten minutes of arguing, we had to give up. We were so close! How could we tell Amber what we knew?

'Come on,' Abs said. 'Let's get a drink and work out our next plan.'

Soph and I agreed this was our only option. We trailed off miserably to the hospital café. Everyone else had drifted off too. The gardens were almost empty now. The café was full of patients though, and their families. We bought some drinks and headed out to sit on a bench outside before getting the bus home.

'So, what's the plan, Stan?' I asked.

'Talk to Amber,' said Abs.

'Yes, I know *that*, but how?'

'By going over there, *now*!' Abs said, leaping up and running off.

Good grief. What was she up to now? Soph and I peered after her to see that she was talking to some girl. It was Amber! We ran over to them.

'So, we met this Poppy lookalike,' Abs was saying as me and Soph panted up to them. Amber was squirming and trying to escape, but Abs had her backed against a wall. She can be seriously forceful when she wants to be.

'Yeah, and she said she'd been really busy recently,' I said.

Amber's eyes darted towards me and then she looked at the ground.

'And Poppy and you have been all over the papers in the past few weeks,' Abs continued, 'and –'

'And then I found that Reflections business card,' Soph said proudly. 'It fell out of your bag the other day.'

'We did think someone had set you up. But we know you're unhappy and we want to know what's going on,' I said.

The others nodded. Abs had her arms folded and looked very stern.

Amber sort of slumped, and then sighed. 'Fine. I may as well tell you. I thought you'd put two and two together when I couldn't find the Reflections card. I hired the fake Poppy.'

'But why?' Abs asked.

'Because I'm desperate. Desperate to get out of The Gems!'

We all gasped in shock. Desperate to leave The Gems? But they were doing so well. It seemed mad to want to leave.

'Why?' I spluttered.

'You're just hitting the big time!' Abs said.

Amber laughed bitterly. 'I know. But I don't like it. We're not known for the kind of music I want to be known for. When I formed the band with Rach and Carly, our music was really different to what we perform now.'

'But you still write it?' I said.

'Yeah, but they turn it into "pop" in the studio. That was my dad's decision. When he started managing us, he could see the pop thing would go down well. Three girls, same outfits, dance routines . . .' Amber shrugged. 'He was right, too. We have done well. And it's still our own music – just produced in a different way. But I'm not happy. I haven't been for a while. And I want out.'

'Have you told him this?' Soph asked.

'I've tried. But he never listens. He's got his plans for The Gems, and that's what he's obsessed with.' Amber wrapped her arms round herself.

'So, what's Poppy got to do with this?' I asked, confused.

Amber looked embarrassed. 'Well, I thought if I got into trouble a lot, and ruined our squeaky-clean image, Dad would get cross and throw me out of the band. After all, his plan for it is bigger than just me. Then I would be free to write the music I want to, and go it alone.' She looked all wistful when she said this.

'So you paid this Poppy lookalike to have a feud with you?' Abs said.

'Yes. I knew that the real Poppy would just think it was the papers making things up again, like they always do. But actually, it was the fake one saying all those things. I told her to.'

I was shocked. 'But what about when you met the real Poppy? You were always at the same parties.'

'Yeah, well, she thought it was the media inventing it. She didn't care. And she loved it anyway. All publicity is good publicity, remember.'

Amber grinned suddenly.

'So did your plan work?' Soph asked. 'Is your dad going to kick you out of The Gems?'

'No, not yet, anyway,' Amber said miserably. 'He's lined up more and more appearances for us.'

'And what about Rach and Carly? What will they do if you go it alone? You're best friends!' I said.

'Oh, they'll be all right,' Amber said, looking down. 'They love what's going on. They love the lifestyle and the money and the glamorous photo shoots . . .'

'But they must know you're unhappy,' Abs said. 'I'd know if Rosie or Soph was unhappy.'

I grinned at her.

Amber sighed again. 'Yeah, I suppose they do, but we haven't really talked about it. They don't want to rock the boat.'

'But –' I began. I couldn't believe Amber's friends would let her be unhappy. Even if they did have to give up lives of luxury, fame, being celebs, getting free stuff and earning loads of money. Er, well, actually, maybe I could believe it . . .

'I didn't know what to do!' Amber said, her eyes welling up. 'No one listens to me, and Dad's so controlling. He just doesn't understand!'

I put an arm round her. 'You've got to talk to him again, Amber,' I said.

Amber started to cry. Abs took her hand. 'Look, Amber, I'm sure he'll listen to you –'

'Amber! There you are!' Her father's loud voice suddenly appeared behind us. He was striding across the hospital entrance, followed by Rach and Carly. 'Where have you been? And what's going on?'

Amber sobbed again, hiding her head in my shoulder.

'Amber!' he barked. 'What's all this about?'

Chapter Nine

Amber's dad was now looming over us. He had his hands on his hips and was glaring at us. My heart was banging in my chest. What was he going to do?

'Erm, Mr Smith,' Abs began nervously, 'We were just talking to Amber, and –'

Amber uncurled herself from my shoulder. 'No,' she said, looking at Abs. 'It's about time I explained.'

'Amber, what are you talking about and what's all this about?' her dad said. 'Have these girls been upsetting you?' He moved a step closer, and I shrank back against the wall. He was being seriously scary.

'No, no!' Amber said. 'They've been helping me. You see, I've been really unhappy. For a long time, actually, Dad.'

'Look, we don't have time for this,' her dad said. 'We've got to go. You need to rehearse for the next gig. Come on.' He went to take Amber by the arm, but she sidestepped away from him.

'No, Dad. You need to listen to me.' She was looking her dad right in the eye.

He sighed and folded his arms. 'Fine. Go on then, I'm listening.'

'Yes, tell us what's going on,' said Rach, smiling at Amber.

Amber took a deep breath. 'Well, you know how there's been all this stuff about how me and Poppy Carlton hate each other?'

Her dad waved a hand dismissively. 'Tabloid rubbish,' he said.

'Well, no, actually. I *did* say those things. And I paid a Poppy lookalike to say the stuff about me,' Amber said.

Rach and Carly looked shocked. 'But why?' Carly asked.

'So Dad would chuck me out of The Gems,' Amber said in a small voice.

'*What?*' Rach exploded. '*Why??!*'

'Were you *that* unhappy?' asked Carly.

Amber nodded. 'Don't get me wrong. I love you girls, and I'm so pleased we're doing well. But I don't like the pop image we've got. And I don't feel like it's *our* band any more.' She glanced at her dad, who was staring at her, looking confused.

Carly and Rach were nodding sympathetically.

'You should have told us,' Rach said.

'Yeah. We could have talked about it,' Carly said. 'Surely we know each other well enough to talk about stuff like this?'

'We're like sisters!' Rach said.

'I can't believe you were so stupid!' her dad said angrily. 'You could have ruined everything! All that stuff in the papers with you looking like an idiot!'

Amber flinched and looked at her friends. It was pretty obvious her dad was the reason she hadn't been able to tell them. Poor Amber! I grabbed Soph's arm and squeezed it. I could always tell *my* friends how I was feeling.

'I know, but I thought, well, all publicity's good publicity,' Amber said bravely, ignoring her dad. 'I could see how much you two were enjoying it all, and I didn't want to ruin your careers. I thought if Dad chucked me out, it wouldn't affect you or our record sales. Not in a bad way, anyway.' She looked at her father again. He still looked pretty angry. 'I mean, loads of bands have changed members and the band still goes on to be successful.'

'So, when you say you don't like the pop image, what were you thinking of instead?' Rach asked.

'Yeah,' Carly said. 'We can do different stuff. Why not?'

Amber smiled at her timidly and began rummaging in her bag. 'Well, I've been writing some new lyrics,' she said. 'I've got them here somewhere . . .'

'We could do different routines, too,' Carly suggested.

'Or no dance routine at all,' Amber said, looking up with a wicked glint in her eye.

Rach and Carly laughed. 'Yeah, OK!'

'Here we are,' Amber said, walking over to a low wall and spreading out some paper on top of it. 'I've got a song here with an R 'n' B feel. Look –'

Rach and Carly crowded round her, and the three of them began reading the lyrics out, and tapping the wall in rhythm.

Me, Abs and Soph looked at each other, and then at Amber's dad. He seemed a bit lost as his band ignored him. He sighed.

'It looks like he'll have to listen to them a bit more in future,' I whispered as we tiptoed towards the hospital exit. 'It's three against one now!'

'Three heads are always better than one,' Abs replied. 'That's why we solve so many mysteries.'

'It helps that your brain is the size of a planet though, Abs,' Soph said.

'Au contraire, mon frère. *We* played vital roles as well,' I protested. 'I found the lookalikes site, and you found the business card, Soph.'

'Yeah, true,' she said. 'Who needs you, Abs?'

'Ha!' Abs laughed, punching her in the arm. 'Very funny.'

We walked out to the bus stop, happy that our job was done.

Chapter Ten

Months later, I was watching telly with Nan when my phone rang. It was a number I didn't recognise.

'Hello, Rosie Parker speaking,' I said in a posh voice. Well, you never know who it might be. It could have been the editor of some stylish magazine calling to say they'd seen my articles in *Star Secrets* and they wanted to offer me a job, based in London, and really well paid. I'd have to say, well, I should probably finish my education first, but if you can keep the job on ice for a few years, then I'm yours. I'd be delighted to accept . . .

'Rosie?' said a female voice. 'It's Amber!'

Amber? Amber? Sacrebleu – it was Amber from The Gems! 'Oh, hi, Amber!' I practically shouted. Nan looked at me crossly. I was interrupting her favourite programme. I ran upstairs to my room. 'Hi, how are you?'

Amber laughed. 'I'm really well, thanks. How are you and Soph and Abs?'

'Oh, yeah, we're fine. You know. Same old stuff. School, mostly. How come you've got my number?'

'Oh, I got it from Fleetwich FM,' Amber said.

Right. I'd given it to them when we'd won the competition to interview The Gems. That felt like ages ago now. Since then, they'd fired their manager, Amber's dad, and had spent ages working on their new sound. Me, Abs and Soph had been following the stories about them. There'd been loads of stuff about the split from Mr Smith. Amber refused to talk about her dad in interviews, but I had to ask what had happened to him.

'Listen, I know I can trust you not to tell anyone, Rosie,' said Amber. 'But the reason he was so pushy with the band was because he needed money.'

'So wasn't he interested in The Gems at all?' I asked.

Amber sighed. 'He was interested, but he kind of got side tracked by his money troubles. It's all sorted now, though,' she chirped. 'And we're fine with each other.'

Me, Abs and Soph agreed it was a good idea to keep your family separate from your job. I mean, I *never* want my mum to be involved in anything I do. Although Soph said when she becomes a fashion designer, she's so going to get Penny to use Sophie McCoy clothes in fashion shoots.

In all the stories about The Gems, Amber looked much happier than before and there were loads of pictures of the three band members together now. They were never wearing the same thing, but their new style looked really funky. And they looked like friends again!

Anyway, then The Gems had been in the studio for *ages* and we were desperate to hear their latest songs.

'How's it going? How's the song-writing going? Are you still talking to your dad?' I gabbled.

Amber laughed. 'Yeah, it's all great. Actually, I'm calling to tell you we're ready to release our new album! It's really exciting. We've been working really hard – and we've written all the songs.'

'Oh, cool!' I said.

'We're really pleased with it. It sounds more rock 'n' roll than our last one,' Amber said. 'And guess what the title is?'

'Um . . . er . . .' I said lamely, unable to think of anything. '"The Gemstones Rock"?'

'Erm, no,' Amber said slowly. 'Although I see what you did there. No, it's called *Reflections*.'

I giggled. 'Brilliant! That's so funny. I've got to tell the others!'

'We thought you'd like it. A little in-joke that only the six of us will get!' Amber laughed.

'Coolissimo!' I said.

I heard a voice in the background say, 'Who's that?'

'It's Rosie,' Amber said. 'Do you wanna say hi? . . . Rosie, it's Rach.'

'Hi, Rosie!' Rach said. 'How are you?'

'Great! I can't wait to hear your new album!' I said.

'Yeah, it's pretty good, even though we say so ourselves,' Rach said. 'Hey, Carly wants to have a quick word.'

'Hi, Rosie!' Carly said.

Wow, all of The Gems in one phone call! 'Hey, Carly!' I said. 'Sounds like you've been busy.'

'Yup. Amber's a real slave-driver,' Carly joked. 'Listen, we've got to go and sign copies of the album. Here's Amber again. See ya!'

After a moment, Amber came on the phone again. 'Well, gotta go, Rosie. But thanks for everything. You guys were so helpful. Without you, we wouldn't have this album. Tell the others, too. Take care! Bye!'

'Bye, Amber. Bye!' I said as she put the phone down.

Wow, how awesome was *that*? An album title

that only me, Abs and Soph knew the story behind. I had to tell the others.

I got online and instant-messaged them:

NosyParker: Guess who just called me?

FashionPolice: Amanda Hawkins?

NosyParker: Quelle horreur! No. Guess again.

CutiePie: Bella from *Star Secrets* magazine?

NosyParker: No. Amber from The Gems!!!

FashionPolice: You lie!

NosyParker: Si, si, signorina. She told me they've just finished their new album. And guess what it's called?

CutiePie: Oh, don't start that again. Just tell us!

NosyParker: Reflections!!!

FashionPolice: LOL!

CutiePie: LOL!

NosyParker: I know!!! :-)

Even better, a few days later, when we'd started seeing the album cover on posters and in magazines, I got a parcel in the post. The postman had to ring the bell because it wouldn't fit through the letterbox. I heard him at the front door, but really, hello? It was, like, seven in the morning. I rolled over in bed.

Next thing I knew, Nan had turned my light on and was standing over me, saying, 'Rosie, Rosie, Rosie,' like some kind of mad ghost.

'Yes, Nan?' I said politely, sitting up immediately with a smile on my face. No, not really. '*What?*' I said grumpily, pulling the duvet over my head.

'There's a parcel for you, dear,' she said, dumping it on my knees.

Oooh! Now that *was* exciting! I sat up and ripped it open to find three CDs of *Reflections*! There was one for me, one for Soph and one for Abs. And they were signed by The Gems! Fantastissimo!

'What is it?' Nan asked.

'It's The Gems' new album! I've got to listen to it *now*,' I said, leaping up.

'Well, why don't you put it on in the kitchen and we can listen to it over breakfast?' Nan suggested.

'OK,' I agreed. Now that I was awake, I was starving.

As me and Nan went downstairs, I heard Mum open her bedroom door. I was glad I hadn't seen her. I'd had too many mornings of seeing her with bed hair, in her gross pyjamas with the word 'Gold' in gold thread all over them. She insists it's the title of some song by some famous band, but whatever. Those PJs are barfarama.

'Morning!' I sang as I skipped down the stairs.

A surprised, 'Urgh?' was all Mum could manage as she shuffled into the bathroom.

I took the très, très sad *Best of the Eighties* CD out of the player and replaced it with the much cooler *Reflections*. Nan switched on the kettle, so I turned up the volume and danced round the kitchen.

'It's rather loud, isn't it?' Nan yelled.

'It's totally brillissimo, that's what it is,' I shouted back. And it was. It was all guitars and drums and cool vocals. The Gems sounded awesome!

I was dying to tell the girls, and they knew something was up straight away.

'Rosie, you're beaming like a loon,' Abs said when she saw me at the bus stop. 'What's happened?'

'Something très, très fab and marvellissimo!' I said, grinning from ear to ear. 'But I have to tell you when we're with Soph too.'

'Fair enough,' Abs said. 'But please stop smiling like that. You're scaring small children.'

When we got to school, I dragged Abs into our form room. The gorgey Mr Adams wasn't there yet, so I sat them both down in front of me and reached into my bag.

'Ta-dah!' I said proudly, handing them a CD each.

'Oooh!' they squealed, realising what it was. Then, 'Aaah!' they screamed, spotting the signatures on the front.

'We've got them a *whole fortnight* before it's officially released,' I said.

'So we'll be the first people to listen to it, other than The Gems themselves,' Abs breathed.

'And the producer, the sound engineer, the mixer . . .' Soph pointed out. Honestly, ever since we recorded those songs a while back, she thinks she knows all about the whole process.

'Yes, yes and – erm – I've already had a quick listen,' I admitted guiltily. 'But all three of us will have listened to it before anyone else *here*,' I said meaningfully, raising my eyebrows in Amanda Hawkins's direction. She immediately looked away, pretending she wasn't listening.

'Cool!' Soph said.

'And look in the booklet,' I said, wriggling with excitement.

Abs took the booklet out of the case and flicked through it. Then she gasped.

'What?' Soph asked.

'Listen to this,' Abs said. '"For the three best friends who, like us, are as close as sisters: Rosie,

Soph and Abs. Thank you for reminding us to talk to each other about everything. This album wouldn't have happened without you. Love, Amber, Rach and Carly."'

Amanda Hawkins made a retching sound, but we ignored her. I looked at my two best friends. 'They're right, you know,' I said. 'They couldn't have done it without us. And we couldn't have done it without each other.'

'One for all and all for one!' Soph suddenly cried.

'I think we should reflect on that motto,' Abs said. 'Get it? *Reflect?*'

Soph and I groaned and then laughed.

'Time to give that genius brain of yours a rest now,' I said to Abs, 'before you come out with any more *gems.*'

Me and Abs laughed. Soph looked at us blankly. We all linked arms and grinned at each other.

'As The Gems would say, best friends rock!' I said.

Soph's Style Tips

Find out how to make a rockin' bag, just like style guru Soph's!

YOU WILL NEED:

- A cotton shopping bag (the kind you get free to use instead of plastic bags)
- An old T-shirt with a cool picture or logo (hit the charity shops to find old band T-shirts for cheap!)
- Scissors
- Safety pins and badges

1. Cut out the main image from your old T-shirt. If your cotton bag has writing on it that you want to cover up, make sure that the section of T-shirt you cut is big enough to cover it.

2. Lay the piece of T-shirt on to the bag, then pin it in place using the safety pins and badges. Et voilà! A rockin' bag that Amber would be proud of!

Fact File

NAME: Amber Smith

AGE: 18

STAR SIGN: Aquarius

HAIR: Long and blonde

EYES: Blue

LOVES: Writing her own music

HATES: Being told what to do

LAST SEEN: Being interviewed on MTV about 'Reflections' getting to number one!

MOST LIKELY TO SAY: The new Avril, moi? Nah, I'm the new Amber! Avril may rock, but I rock harder!

WORST CRINGE EVER: When she paid Poppy Carlton's lookalike to shout, 'Amber doesn't wash her socks!' across a celeb-filled cinema at a movie premiere. She went red from head to toe and thought maybe this time she had taken things a step too far . . .

Megastar

Everyone has blushing blunders - here are some from your Megastar Mysteries friends

Rosie

Last year, Soph made me a crazy customised birthday present (what I thought was a top). I was très impressed that she'd put so much effort into a pressie for little old me, and told her I loved it. But when I got it home and had another look at it, there were so many bits of ribbon, zips and slits that I didn't know how to put it on! I eventually squeezed into it and, even though it felt a bit tight in places, I thought it looked OK. But when I arrived at the school disco in my new creation, Soph's jaw dropped and Abs fell about laughing. 'Erm, why are you wearing the bag I made you as a top, Rosie?' asked Soph. Doh! That's the last time I try and pull off anything more fashionable than a pair of jeans!

Sophie

When we went up to London to see The Gems I knew I had to look my best, so I packed all of my favourite clothes into a smart holdall to work out some cool outfits on the train. I spread everything out over the seat and got in a right fluster trying to stuff it all back in when the train arrived in London. I staggered along with my massive bag all the way to my Aunt Penny's house, but imagine how red my cheeks went when I plopped my bag down in her hall only to notice a pair of my knickers caught in the zip. They must have been waving like a flag the whole way there!

Cringes

Amber

When we perform as The Gems we normally wear this really cool sparkly eyeshadow, but one day I was determined to look different. I begged the make-up lady to do rock-chick style black eye make-up on me. The other girls weren't sure about it, but I thought it looked awesome. Only problem was, when we got on stage and started jumping about, my make-up began to run down my cheeks. The more it ran, the more I rubbed my eyes and the worse it looked! My panda eyes were all over *Star Secrets* the next week – cringe!

Mr Adams

Believe it or not, I'm a big fan of school dinners. One day, I got chatting to the school cook and told her all about this delicious chocolatey, custardy pudding I used to eat when I was at school. The next day, I popped my head into the dining room to see what was on the menu and saw 'Mr Adam's Chocolate Surprise' written on the board. The cook had kindly recreated my favourite pud! I couldn't wait to try it, and loads of the pupils lined up to have a taste too. But when I had a taste, it was disgusting – cold and thick with a puckered skin over it. Yuck! All the kids thought I was a total weirdo for eating it, plus I had to finish my portion and tell the cook how much I loved it so I didn't look rude!

Pam

I was so excited when I heard that my Rosie and her friends were going up in the Fleetwich FM helicopter. I asked my friend Gerry to come round, and we waited in the garden with a nice cup of tea in the best china to mark the occasion. Suddenly, I leapt out of my chair and started waving madly. There she is!' I cried, craning my neck up to the sky. 'I'd recognise my Rosie anywhere!' 'Um, I think you'll find that's a pigeon, Pam,' said Gerry, just as what I had thought was the helicopter dropped something white and sloppy on to the toe of my slipper. A pigeon helicopter and a poopy slipper all at once – double cringe!

What's Your Band Destiny?

So you wanna be a music star? Take the quiz to find out what kind of band would suit you best!

1. What's your musical instrument of choice?

a. Something rocky, like the drums or the guitar
b. My voice – I reckon singing is ace!
c. Who cares – just chuck on a CD and get dancing!

2. Where do you dream of performing?

a. A stadium in front of millions of screaming fans
b. On a sunny beach
c. In the coolest club in town

3. What's your favourite party outfit?

a. Jeans and a T-shirt – maybe one I customised myself!
b. Anything really colourful
c. Something that matches my best mate's outfit!

4. What did you do in the last school play?

a. Fell over on stage and make a complete fool of myself!
b. Played the lead part – everyone thought I was great!
c. Got stuck into the dance routines – brilliant!

5. What kind of animal are you most like?

a. I love being cosy, just like a cat
b. I'm a little bit cheeky and loads of fun, like a monkey
c. I'm like a puppy – full of energy and friendly

6. What do your favourite trainers look like?

a. They're muddy and full of holes, but I love them!
b. Sparkly and colourful
c. Bright white and sporty

How did you score?

Mostly As: You're a rockin' rock chick!

Just like Amber, you're destined to be a rock 'n' roll star! You like to be a little bit different from everyone else and don't mind standing out in the crowd, so jumping about with a guitar sounds right up your street!

Mostly Bs: Can we call you little Miss Pop?

You're one cute popstress who always has a smile on her face, just like Rach! You're always hanging around with your mates anyway, so why not get together and form a pop band? You've probably already got the cheeky nicknames sorted, so it's time to get working on those vocals!

Mostly Cs: Hey, dancing diva!

Do you ever keep your feet still?! A dance act would suit you perfectly cos you're always on the move and love getting dressed up in crazy outfits. Listening to any kind of music makes you want to dance, and the louder the beat, the wilder you get, just like Carly!

Have a super

Find out how to make your next party full of stars!

Awesome Invites

Collect some old CDs (ones that come free in the newspaper are perfect) and write the details of your party on the shiny side with a permanent pen. Poptastic!

Play DJ

Borrow an MP3 player and load it up with pop music. Then set it to play on random and bingo, you've got yourself the perfect soundtrack! Just make sure your mum doesn't add any of her old faves to it – Rosie's mum would definitely try and squeeze some cringey eighties tunes in!

Celebrity Party

Famous Fashion

If you don't fancy dress-as-a-star style fancy dress, why not stock up on cheapo sunglasses at the pound shop and hand them out to your guests when they arrive? You'll all look like celebs in no time!

Superstar Snacks

Feed your new celeb chums with star-shaped sarnies (your fave sandwiches cut into cute shapes with biscuit cutters), superstar strawberries (strawberries with a bowl of choccy spread to dip them in) and celebrity celery (celery sticks with yummy dips). Bribe your little bro or sis into passing round plates of food (which you should call canapés) for an added touch of luxury!

Pam's Problem Page

Never fear, Pam's here to sort you out!

Dear Pam,

My dad is trying to make me stay in this pop band that he's mad about, but I'm not enjoying it anymore. He won't listen me, and now I feel like I'll do anything to get out! If I get into trouble then maybe he will get angry and force me to leave. What do you think, Pam? Shall I do it?

Amber

Pam says: Oh, dear, you have got yourself into a pickle, haven't you? But if there's one thing I've learned from all my years of watching *Murder, She Wrote*, it's that the baddies always lose. Don't be tempted to get yourself or anyone else in trouble, love, it's just not worth it. I'll tell you what, you get your bad dad round to my house for a cup of tea and a biscuit and I think I can win him over. It's amazing what a nice sit-down in a comfy chair and a garibaldi biscuit can do, you know.

Can't wait for the next
book in the series?
Here's a sneak preview of

Polly

Chapter One

The day before half-term is one of my favourites – it totally rocks! So far, all we'd done this time was mess around, and none of the teachers seemed to care. Even Mr Adams couldn't keep his mind on long division.

'So what's everyone getting up to during the holidays?' he asked, throwing aside a maths book and smiling at the class. 'Anything exciting?'

Abs let out a very un-Abs-like squeak, and me and Soph giggled. 'Exciting' didn't even come close to describing the fabuloso time we had planned!

I was just about to tell Mr Adams all about it, when Amanda Hawkins started flicking her hair around like she was in a shampoo advert. Amanda Hawkins has two hobbies – showing off and being mean. She always flicks her hair when she's about to say something smug. It's très annoying, let me tell you.

'I'm going to Jersey for the week,' Amanda boasted in a show-offy voice. 'My uncle has a hotel there. In fact, my uncle's hotel is actually the largest on the island. Five star, of course.'

'But of course!' I whispered under my breath.

Amanda turned around and glared at me. 'So what are you doing, Rosie Parker? Staying in boring Borehurst?'

'No, no. Me, Abs and Soph are going to stay at the Hotel Kesterton in London,' I said, sounding très sophisticated. 'James Piper's staying there while he rehearses for his new play, and the hotel manager has booked my mum's band to sing for him.'

A stunned silence fell over the class and Abs stifled a giggle.

So, OK, it totally sounded like one of my celeb-fuelled daydreams, but it really was true! My mum's Bananarama tribute band, the Banana Splits, had been chosen to play for James Piper. Oui, mes amis! *The* James Piper! The hugely talented, not to mention swoonsome, Hollywood actor! It was like I'd wandered into a parallel universe, where Mum's cringey music was actually cool. It was très weird.

Amanda's eyes slid from me, to Abs, to Soph and back to me again. Her mean little mind was obviously in overdrive.

'That's a lie, Rosie Parker!' she practically hissed. 'Why would your mum's tribute band be asked to play for James Piper? Get real.'

'I think you'll find that James is a big fan of eighties music and eighties tribute bands,' Soph explained.

Abs waved this week's copy of *Star Secrets* in the air, then started reading from an interview. '"James has always loved eighties music",' she read. '"It reminds him of his happy early teenage years with his younger brother, David, on their family's farm in Texas. The farm was so remote, the boys could only get two radio stations. One was country and western, which they both hated, and the other station played chart hits. James could listen all day long! He never got tired of that eighties vibe".'

'But I suppose if you're never going to meet him, you don't really need to know that,' Soph said in Amanda's direction.

'Well, that's very true, Soph,' I said, smiling kindly at Amanda, who had gone very red. 'Have you heard of the Hotel Kesterton, Amanda?'

'It's five star, of course,' Abs added with a glint in her eye.

* * *

It seemed about a million years until the next day. Nan came to wave us off at the train station, which was a good thing as we needed all the help we could get with Soph's massivo suitcase.

'I wanted to cover all fashion eventualities,' Soph explained. Not that she needed to explain herself to us. We're totally used to her fashionista ways.

'I find it's the shoes that make bags heavy,' Mum said helpfully.

Soph looked at her case thoughtfully. 'I only brought twelve pairs,' she said. 'Oh, and a couple of pairs of boots, and some sandals.'

Me and Abs started to giggle.

'If I didn't know you better, Sophie, I'd say you had a dead body in here!' Nan chuckled.

Honestly! Nan is always coming out with things like that. She watches waaay too many murder mysteries for her own good, if you ask me.

'I can't understand why you girls don't wear synthetic fabrics. They're easy to pack, light and funky,' Mum told Soph.

Hmmm. Sometimes it can be hard being the only one in the Parker household with a grip on reality. Nan thinks she's Jessica Fletcher from *Murder, She Wrote* and Mum reckons synthetic fabrics are cool. What chance do I have? I mean, I actually had to explain who James Piper was to Mum! Can you believe it? I just don't see how she could have missed all the stories about him in the paper. His brother's car accident last year was headline news, for, like, months. Zut alors, it was on the telly! The whole world held their breath while James sat by David's bedside in Los Angeles. It was très awful. At first, the doctors said that it was touch-and-go whether he'd make it, but little by little, David got better. That's how James met April, his gorgeous fiancée. She was one of his brother's nurses.

And just this week, the papers had been full of more stories about James. This time they were about his new play, *The Good Turn*, and his close friendship with British actress Polly McAllistair. Their fabuloso chemistry on stage had sparked pages and pages of gossip. All the papers were speculating about whether they were having an affair behind April's back. It was big news! But had Mum heard about any of it? Nah. Nope. Nada.

Luckily for Mum, I'd bought some press cuttings for her to read on the train. I might not have been able to drag her out of the eighties, but at least I could fill in a few of the missing years.

PIPER IS A SELL-OUT!

It's official, James Piper is set to star in the West End play, *A Good Turn*. But if you want to book tickets, you're already too late! They sold out as soon as the news was announced. We caught up with April, James's gorgeous fiancée, to find out more. 'Everyone with a ticket is in for a treat,' she told us. 'I've watched all the rehearsals and I have to say, this is the best role James has ever played.'

TWO OF A KIND

James Piper and British actress Polly McAllistair have been getting on like a house on fire during rehearsals for *A Good Turn*. According to our celebrity spy, the on-stage chemistry between James and Polly is sizzling hot. Could romance be on the horizon for these stage sweethearts? And what does April think of her fiancé's relationship with Polly? Watch this space, readers!

When our taxi drew up at the Hotel Kesterton, we were practically beside ourselves with excitement. The lobby was totally coolissimo! It was bigger than our school hall and pure white, with a très chic glass sculpture hanging from the ceiling.

Mum went to the reception desk to check us in while we perched on some white leather sofas and tried to look casual.

'Sacrebleu!' whispered Soph. 'It's James and April!'

'Where? Where?' Me and Abs jumped to our feet and looked around wildly. Sure enough, there were James and April, walking across the glittering lobby, right in front of us! April looked even more petite in real life. The light bounced off her glossy brown hair as she giggled at something James was saying.

A second later, Polly McAllistair stepped out of the lift. She looked just as gorgeous as April, though she was tall and blonde and had a totally different style. We held our breath, half-expecting there to be some kind of showdown, but April and Polly greeted each other with a kiss on both cheeks as if they were perfectly friendly. We shrugged at each other as they disappeared into the restaurant.

'Well,' Abs sighed, 'it just goes to show you can't believe everything you read in the papers.'

※　※　※

We spent the next couple of hours unpacking and exploring the hotel. Me, Soph and Abs had a totally cool room. It was all pink and silver and there was even a seating area arranged around a chrome fireplace. Abs-the-cynic was convinced it was fake but Mum wouldn't let us light a fire to test it out. There was a solar-powered laptop and a huge-issimo telly too. Mum had the adjoining room with a connecting door so she could keep an eye on us.

Later, as we sat in the restaurant waiting for the Banana Splits to come on, I started feeling a bit wobbly. It was kind of hard to believe that James Piper was going to listen to Mum voluntarily. Don't get me wrong, I was totally proud of her . . . in theory . . . but the pride was kind of overshadowed by a severe attack of embarrassment. I mean, no girl wants to watch her mother strutting her 'funky stuff' – even if there are celebrities in the room. *Especially* if there are celebrities in the room! It was too much of a cringe-fest. As Mum's band took to the stage I couldn't bear to watch.

'Open your eyes, Rosie! James and April are totally loving it!' coaxed Abs. I hid behind my hands and groaned.

Abs nudged me in the ribs. 'Open. Your. Eyes.'

'No way, José!' I cried, squeezing my eyes even tighter.

'Go on,' soothed Abs. 'Everyone's enjoying it

. . . all the older ones, anyway.'

I didn't even want to imagine what was happening! Seriously!

'Is Mum making them dance? Argh! Don't tell me. I don't want to know.'

'Open your eyes, mon amie. Everyone's dancing,' Soph told me.

'No!' I said.

'Yes,' said Soph. 'It's really cool.'

'Au contraire, mon frère,' I said, shaking my head. 'Not possible.'

'Honestly, Rosie! It's totally not that bad!' Abs insisted.

'That's easy for you to say – she's not your mum!' I said, darkly.

Abs and Soph grabbed my hands and gently pulled them away from my face. I squinted through the smoke-machine clouds and saw James pulling April and Polly on to the dance floor. The whole restaurant was boogying to the Banana Splits. It was cringey. It was cool. It was weird.

After that, everything seemed to speed up.

Mum shimmied her way through Bananarama's greatest hits in what seemed like record time. Then suddenly she was sitting at our table sipping water and fanning herself with a dessert menu. I sat there, stunned, while people rushed up to congratulate her and the other members of the band. I was just thinking that life couldn't get any more surreal when Polly McAllistair came over and shook Mum's hand. Seriously! I am not joking!

'That was fabulous!' smiled Polly. 'I haven't danced that much in years!'

Within minutes, Mum and Polly were totally chatting like old friends.

'This is my daughter, Rosie, and these are her friends, Abs and Soph,' Mum said as we shook hands with Polly.

'You must be so proud of your mum,' smiled Polly.

'Er, yes. I'm glad you enjoyed the show,' I said, feeling dazed.

'I don't suppose you'd give us your autograph?' Mum asked.

Me, Abs and Soph grinned at each other – we'd all been dying to ask the same thing! Polly signed our restaurant menus while we told her how much we'd enjoyed her last film. Then she asked us all about ourselves and we chatted for ages.

'When James and April come back, I'll make sure you get their autographs too,' Polly told us. 'I think April wanted to call LA, so she's nipped upstairs to use the phone, and I don't know where James has got to – he's probably chatting with the play's director.'

We talked for a few more minutes, then Polly told us she had to go.

'She's so gorgeous close-up,' said Soph, as Polly disappeared into the crowd.

'She's a lovely person too,' I added. 'Totally down to earth.'

We talked about Polly for a while and then ordered some fizzy drinks. While we waited for them to come, we debated how well James Piper measured up to Maff, the gorgey singer from Fusion. As I pointed out, it was hard to compare them, because James was *much* more mature.

Suddenly, there was a commotion over by the door. The main lights whooshed on and we sat there, blinking in the glare.

'I apologise for the interruption to your evening,' the restaurant manager said into the stage microphone. 'I'm afraid there has been a burglary in the hotel. Expensive jewellery belonging to James Piper's fiancée has been stolen. I'd like to ask everybody to stay calm. The police are on their way and they'd like to interview everyone who is at the hotel this evening, so please remain in the restaurant.'

Me, Abs and Soph gawped at each other in shock. Sacrebleu! We were slap-bang in the middle of a celebrity mystery again!